Look what people are saying about fan favorite Hope Tarr...

"4.5 Stars, Top Pick! Sparkling characters, well-developed emotion and first-rate writing make this a great story."
—*Romantic Times BOOKreviews* on *Strokes of Midnight*

"Readers who enjoy 'naughtier' books with a strong plot and well-developed characters will positively adore this book."
—*CK2S Kwips and Kritiques* on *The Haunting*

"A delightful, intriguing mix of past and present, love and betrayal, *The Haunting* by Hope Tarr is sure to find its way into your heart. Add this one to your to-buy list. 4 1/2 Stars!"
—*Cataromance*

"Vivid, well-rounded characters and lively dialogue...an excellent finale to the Men of Roxbury House trilogy."
—*Romantic Times BOOKreviews* on *Untamed*

"Hope Tarr's books always deliver that emotional kick that makes me crave more."
—Barbara Vey, *Publishers Weekly*, "Beyond Her Book" blog, on *Enslaved*

Blaze™

Dear Reader,

I am thrilled to help launch the first historical for Harlequin's Blaze line. My bold chieftain heroine, Brianna MacLeod, embodies the modern-day moxie of a Harlequin Blaze heroine set against the breathtakingly romantic backdrop of fifteenth-century Scotland. As for my hero, Ewan Fraser, a hunk with a heart of gold is a true treasure in any era.

Brianna's beloved castle is loosely based on Dunvegan Castle on the Isle of Skye, the seat of Clan MacLeod for more than seven centuries and likely the oldest continuously inhabited castle in Europe. Read on as Brianna recounts the legend behind the bull on the clan crest. To learn more about the fascinating history of Clan MacLeod and Dunvegan Castle, visit the Web site at www.dunvegancastle.com. Until next time...

Wishing you a summer filled with fairy-tale dreams come true and sexy second chances.

Hope Tarr
www.hopetarr.com

HOPE TARR
Bound To Please

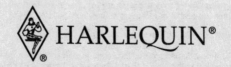

TORONTO • NEW YORK • LONDON
AMSTERDAM • PARIS • SYDNEY • HAMBURG
STOCKHOLM • ATHENS • TOKYO • MILAN • MADRID
PRAGUE • WARSAW • BUDAPEST • AUCKLAND

ISBN-13: 978-0-373-79411-9
ISBN-10:   0-373-79411-8

BOUND TO PLEASE

ABOUT THE AUTHOR

Hope Tarr is an award-winning author of multiple contemporary and historical romance novels. *Bound To Please* is her tenth book and the first historical for Harlequin's Blaze line. When not writing, Hope indulges her passions for feline rescue and historic preservation. To enter her monthly contest or check out the latest news on her "semi blog," visit her online at www.hopetarr.com.

Books by Hope Tarr
HARLEQUIN BLAZE

Don't miss any of our special offers. Write to us at the following address for information on our newest releases.

Harlequin Reader Service
U.S.: 3010 Walden Ave., P.O. Box 1325, Buffalo, NY 14269
Canadian: P.O. Box 609, Fort Erie, Ont. L2A 5X3

To Brenda Chin, editor extraordinaire.

1

Martinmas Fair, November 11, 1450
Saint Andrews, County Fife, Scotland

BRIANNA SLIPPED OUT OF the covered market building where the fair day feast was under way. Though she was a stranger here, indistinguishable from the other fair-goers, the bounty offered rivaled any banquet served to honored guests in her da's great hall. Even with her belly so full her sides felt close to splitting, thinking of the delicacies weighing down the trestle tables within—the delectable tarts and custards, fancy nuts and cheeses, and flaky pasty pies both sweet and savory—made her mouth water. The richly spiced foods had left her with a powerful thirst, which she'd quenched with cup upon cup of the free-flowing, honey-sweetened milk. Now her brimming bladder would no longer be denied. Future laird or no, she was still human. Nature's call cared not for rank or bloodline.

Hugging her plaid about her shoulders, she left the market cross and headed down the High Gate in search of privacy, her footfalls nearly soundless on the mud-packed lane, her way lit by tarred torches and bracketed by empty market stalls. Flute music drew her toward the stable. The plaintive song stopped just as she approached the half-cocked door. Deciding it must have come from off in the distance, after all, she darted a glance over her shoulder and then slipped inside, pulling the door closed behind her.

A lantern hung on a peg on the far wall, its feeble light scarcely strong enough to tunnel through the shadows. Brianna shivered, the darkness resurrecting childhood fears of witches with warty noses, demons that poked you with their pitchforks, and goblins that stole naughty bairns from their beds at night. She shuffled toward the light, arms outstretched to ward off falling. Her palms scraped the rough wall. Anchoring herself to the corner, she lifted her skirts and squatted. Ah, sweet relief…

"You piss a rare fine stream for a girl."

Brianna started. Heart hammering, she yanked down her skirts and leaped up, searching the shadows.

"Up here." The husky tones beckoning her to look above belonged to a youth, not a grown man, and certainly not an otherworldly creature.

Face burning, Brianna craned her neck and squinted. A pair of long-boned legs swung from the beam above, the big booted feet barely clearing her head. The feet belonged to a boy of twelve or so with wavy, shoulder-length dark hair, laughing eyes and a wooden flute held in one broad hand.

From his perch he must have gotten a good glimpse of her woman's parts. Six months ago that wouldn't have bothered her a bit, but since the start of her courses, she'd developed a new modesty. Shameful heat seared her cheeks as though she stood too near a fire.

Determined to regain her lost dignity, she lifted her chin and speared him with a deliberate dagger glare. "You should have made your presence known."

He jumped down, landing in the straw beside her. "Why? You didn't see fit to announce yours." Straightening, he brushed the hay from his tunic and trousers, both sadly in want of mending, and tucked the flute inside his pocket. "Besides, I was here first."

It was the truth. She had entered uninvited, though the stable was a public place. "It doesna matter. As a future laird, I outrank you."

Instead of being cowed as she'd expected, he threw back his dark head and laughed. Swiping a hand over his eyes, he shook his head as though she were a child and he a grown-up. "Girls canna be lairds."

The statement inflamed Brianna like the striking together of flint and steel. She punched a fist in the air. "I can—and I will. My da swears it will be so, and as he is clan chief, his word is law. Someday I shall be known as The MacLeod."

Before they'd set out on their journey, her father had told her he didn't mean to take another wife. He had four bairns in the kirkyard, her dear mother buried with the last, and he was coming to believe he wasn't meant to beget boys. Before his death, an event Brianna hoped wouldn't come to pass for a very long time, he meant to name her, his sole surviving child, as heir.

The youth rolled his eyes and Brianna was struck by their clear gray, almost opaque color—a trick of the shadows, perhaps, though she didn't think so. "A laird's duties include leading men into battle. A woman can't do that."

The comment hit home. Before setting out, she'd overheard the old gentlemen, her father's trusted councillors, say much the same. "I suppose you've never heard of Joan of Arc, you oaf."

He shrugged his shoulders, broad for a boy of his young years. "That was different. She had visions from the saints—Saints Michael, Catherine and Margaret, to be exact. You don't strike me as likely to be visited by the divine anytime soon."

Brianna bit her lip. She couldn't argue with him there. She'd been getting into scrapes almost since taking her first shaky baby step.

Seizing the upper hand, the boy barreled on. "Besides, you'll have to marry someday and you know what that means. You'll birth bairns. Your belly will grow big as a croft, and you'll be too fat to lead your men into battle unless you want them to waddle like ducks. Your enemies will call the MacLeods Clan Quack-quack."

Brianna stamped her foot in the straw. "They will not."

"Will, too."

No doubt her dear departed mother was wagging an admonishing finger at her from heaven above, but for the moment, Brianna was too angry to care. She balled her fingers into a fist, hauled back—and swung.

Her knuckles met the lad's lean midriff, stony hard despite his lack of years and girth. Such a blow would have felled most boys her age, but to his credit, he held his ground.

"Ouch!" Rubbing his stomach, he stared at her, the crystalline purity of his gaze already rendering her sorry. "I ken you have a temper to match your hair."

Ignoring his reference to her red-gold tresses, presently gathered into a single messy plait, Brianna folded her arms and glared at him. "'Tis your just punishment for speaking out of turn, for you are neither my kinsman nor my equal." She raked her gaze over his common garb with deliberate thoroughness.

He glared at her, his eyes darkening. "For all you ken, I'm a future clan chief myself."

She glanced at the worn plaid gathered about his shoulders and chest. Faded though the fabric was, now that her eyes had adjusted to the low light she made out the pattern of brilliant scarlet interwoven with forest-green, the Fraser colors. Brianna drew back. The Mac-Leods and the Frasers weren't enemies, exactly, but they weren't friends, either. In recent years, MacLeod cattle had been known to "wander" off, particularly around market days. She'd heard the laird had twin sons, Callum and Ewan, two years younger than she and born mere minutes apart, but before now she'd never given that bit of news all that much thought.

Wondering which of the brothers she faced, she asked, "Well, are you?"

He shook his head, gaze clouding. "Nay, my brother Callum is older than I by two minutes. I am Ewan, my father's youngest."

She reached out her hand. "I am Brianna, my father's only." Even resolved to be friendly, she couldn't seem to set aside her pride.

He took it, long fingers furling about hers, his grip firm but gentle and pleasantly warm. "I am pleased to meet you, Brianna of the MacLeods. So what brings a laird's daughter—excuse me, a future laird—to a fair day so far from our island home?"

"I'm helping my da drive our cattle to market, but we bided here to see the fair and celebrate the feast day." She glanced down to her hand, which he still held.

Cheeks coloring, he released her. "Driving cattle to market seems a verra big job for a girl."

She sensed he was deliberately tweaking her again, and yet, as always, the reference to her sex rankled. If only she might have been born a boy, how much simpler life would be. She drew herself up to her full height. Though still growing, she already topped most of the women in her clan and stood on eye level with many boys her age. Despite being her junior, Ewan Fraser stood several inches taller than she.

"I'm not just any girl. I'm the daughter of The MacLeod."

He shook his dark head, daring her with his clear, canny eyes. "Well, you're verra pretty, Brianna of the MacLeods. And you smell like spring flowers."

Meeting his gaze, Brianna felt her heart give a funny little flutter. He must have noticed the perfumed soap with which she'd washed her face and neck and hair— a concoction of crushed cherry blossoms and lavender her nursemaid, Milread, made for her specially.

But even better, he'd called her pretty. She wasn't ugly, certainly, but she'd never before thought of herself as fair. For one thing, she was too tall and too big-boned.

And she was too wide-mouthed for another. And then there was the matter of her hair, the riotous red curls defiant of any plait or coil. Pretty girls were tiny as fairies, with pink pouts and straight flaxen locks that fell below their waists like silk curtains.

"'Tis a pity you're so verra haughty," he added, gaze narrowing.

Caught up as she was in the earlier unexpected compliment, it took her a moment before for the criticism hit home. She'd sat in on a sufficient number of quarterly court days to know that her father always treated the lowliest crofter and the loftiest lord with the same courtesy. Magnus MacLeod's fair-handedness was one of many qualities that had earned him the fierce loyalty of his fellow clansmen. Though Brianna strove to be like him in every way, it seemed she'd failed once again.

She let her shoulders droop. "I suppose I could do with a wee bit more humility." Striving to be more fair-minded, she added, "You can hit me back if you like."

He answered her suggestion with a fierce shake of his head, horror dawning on his lean-featured face. "Nay, I canna."

"Don't be silly, fair is fair." She stuck out her less than slender stomach and braced herself for his blow. "No, really, go to."

Clear gray eyes rested on her face. Despite his mild manners, she sensed the steel in him. "Even if you are a MacLeod, you're still a lassie. My da would have my hide if he found out I'd struck you, and what was left of me my ma would tan. You're verra brave, though." He hesitated. "Do you really think they'll let you be laird?"

For the first time since her father had taken her aside and confided his plans, Brianna felt a seed of doubt take root. "If my da decrees it, then it must be so."

Gaze dropping to their feet, he moved straw about with the toe of one boot. "You'll still have need of a husband, though."

Brianna shrugged. "Aye, I suppose I will." Of all the many things she was looking forward to about being a grown-up, marriage ranked low on her wish list. "I've been betrothed to my cousin Donald since we were weans, but he doesna fancy playing outdoors as I do, and my cat, Muffin, makes him sneeze."

Ewan snapped his head up, a smile spreading over his face. "Marry me instead. I best my brother in nearly all the games. In another few years I'll be old enough to take part in the caber toss with the grown men. Oh, and I like cats well enough." He hesitated, and then added, "Well, at least they don't make me sneeze."

Brianna stared at him, curious and a wee bit flustered. Had she really just received a proposal of marriage? If she must take a husband, certainly Ewan Fraser would suit her far better than her quiet, bookish cousin.

"I'll have to ask my da, but I suppose it'd be all right."

Ewan's smile broadened. "I dinna have anything to serve as a ring, but for a betrothal to be binding, we must exchange something."

She stopped to think about that. The only thing of value she had with her was her short-bladed dirk, a gift from her da on her last saint's day. She was reluctant to give it up.

"A blood oath will serve as well as a gift, mayhap

better." She slid up her skirt and unsheathed the small knife from her stocking. Straightening, she brandished the blade.

Ewan didn't flinch, nor did he exclaim over the handsomeness of the jewel-encrusted hilt as she'd supposed he would. "Here's hoping you ken how to use it."

"Of course I do," she retorted. "To prove it, I'll do mine first."

She turned her left hand palm up. Biting her bottom lip so as not to cry out and shame herself, she dragged the blade tip over the fatty part of her thumb, raising a thin scarlet semicircle. Holding it out, she said, "See?"

She reached for his hand, but he shook his head. "I'll do my own cutting, thank you very much."

Brianna hesitated. Dare she turn over her weapon to a stranger, let alone one belonging to a rival clan? Rival or not, she doubted he would use it to slit her throat— he was only a boy, after all, albeit an uncommonly beautiful and strong one—but what was to keep him from pocketing her prize and running off?

But his steadfast gaze struck down that fleeting thought, stirring something inside her, a queer fluttery feeling taking root in her heart. Whatever Fate held in store for them, Brianna sensed it involved a good deal more than petty theft.

She handed over the knife. "Verra well. Only mind you don't get any ideas about running off. I'm strong as any boy, and I've legs like a rabbit. I wouldn't rest 'til I'd run you to ground, and once I did, it's more than your thumb I'd cut."

The corners of his amazing eyes crinkled in a smile.

"Brianna of the MacLeods, without doubt you're the boldest lass I've ever met."

Brianna found herself smiling back. "Mayhap you should get out more." Never mind that the present journey was the first time she'd set foot on mainland soil.

He took the knife and used the tip to make a deep, semicircular gash, a near mirror image to hers, only deeper. Watching the bubbling blood, she couldn't help but admire how he accomplished the feat with nary a wince.

"There." He handed back the knife.

She reached out with her good hand and took it. Sliding it back inside her stocking, she stretched out her bloodied hand to his, feeling as though they were in a chapel or some other sacred place. They clasped hands, fingers locking, and chafed their joined palms.

Ewan's strangely colored eyes met hers. "I, Ewan Fraser, swear that seven years hence, I shall claim you, Brianna of the MacLeods, as my bride."

Heart skipping, Brianna answered, "I, Brianna MacLeod, swear I will take no husband but you, Ewan Fraser, seven years hence from this day."

She drew her hand away and looked down at the smearing, a sense of awe washing over her. Her blood and Ewan's were as good as one. "We have a pact."

"Not quite yet. We should seal the bargain with a kiss as well." One corner of his mouth kicked up, the lopsided grin at odds with his somber eyes.

Brianna snapped up her head. "A kiss?"

"Aye." He nodded, eyes agleam. "'Tis no ordinary bargain, after all, but a betrothal."

About to enter her fourteenth year, she'd never experienced a grown-up kiss before. Imagining Ewan's full, firm lips taking possession of hers, she felt a queer tingling streaking through her, the sensation part curiosity—and part fear. But as he had displayed such nobility in bearing up to the bloodletting, could she really show less heart?

She leaned in, laid her hands atop his shoulders and matched her mouth to his. The kiss began as soft and gentle as a steady summer shower. Ewan's lips moving over hers were cool and firm, his breath sweet-smelling and freshened with fennel, reminding her of the comfits she'd sampled earlier at the fair. She'd grown up being entertained in her father's great hall by troubadours and balladeers likening a lady's lips to rose petals and her breasts to turtle doves. Until now Brianna hadn't understood what that really meant, let alone what all the fuss was about.

She did now.

Ewan's hands wrapped about her waist, pulling her closer. The kiss deepened. He slid his tongue between her parted lips, and a warm thrumming struck low in her belly, the very spot where the monthly cramping centered. Only what she felt now wasn't pain. It must be that much celebrated sensation—desire.

Brianna jerked back, startled by the wellspring of feelings rising within her. Flushed and flustered, she sent him a shaky smile. "I ken you just might do for a husband, after all."

"Brianna…Brie! Where the devil have you got to, girl?"

Her father's voice ringing outside the stable had Brianna shrinking from adult stature back to childhood once more. She twisted her head toward the door, thankful she'd thought to close it when she'd entered. The MacLeod was slow to anger, but he'd be none too pleased at the prospect of his daughter fraternizing with a Fraser. Were he to find out their dallying had ended with a kiss, he might be sufficiently doubtful of her good judgment and name her other cousin, Hugh, as his heir instead. Seven years her junior, Hugh was scarcely out of leading strings. Still, you never knew.

She swung back to Ewan. Dropping her voice to a whisper, she said, "That's my da. I must go. We set out early on the morrow."

He sent her a sad look and nodded. "Verra well, only mind our pact. When we're grown, we'll wed each other and no one else."

"Aye, I'll mind it well enough." Heart heavy, she turned to the door.

"Brianna, halt."

Heart pumping, she wheeled about. "Aye?"

He held out the flute for her to take. Brianna shook her head. "Nay, Ewan, I canna—"

"Aye, you can." He crossed the straw-covered floor, reached for her hand and pressed the instrument into her palm. "It's not much of a bride gift, but I'll do better when we're grown."

Brianna's fingers curved about the smooth wood, warmed from having been in Ewan's pocket. Never in her life had she been so moved by a gift. "But I dinna ken how to play it."

Ewan seemed to find that funny. His beautiful mouth broke into a broad grin and his eyes, dulled mere moments ago, twinkled like twin stars. "No matter, lass.

Once we're wed, I'll play any tune you fancy." He punctuated the promise with a wink.

Outside, heavy footsteps drew nearer. "Brianna, Brie, answer me, Daughter."

Brianna was canny enough to catch the fear underlying the sharpness in her father's voice. He was worried about her. She dare not tarry any longer.

She stared up at Ewan, feeling as though she was about to bid farewell to a longtime friend rather than a boy she'd met mere minutes ago. "Until we meet again, fare thee well, Ewan Fraser."

"You willna forget, will you, Brie?" His gray-eyed gaze bore into hers.

Feeling close to crying, she shook her head. "Nay, Ewan, I willna forget." She kissed his cheek and then turned and darted out the door.

2

Castle MacLeod, Dunvegan, Isle of Skye
Whitsunday, May 15, Ten Years Later

"I HAVE TAKEN YOUR BROTHER in payment for my husband. An eye for an eye…"

Quill clenched between ink-stained fingers, Brianna, laird of Clan MacLeod, looked up from the kidnapping note and stared out the solar window, searching the nearly cloudless canopy of blue sky, ragged mountain ridge and boulder-bordered loch for inspiration, or better yet, a sign. But for once, her home's bold beauty failed to inspire her. A salt-scented breeze blew inside the open casement, drying the freshly spent ink and fluttering the edges of the unfinished letter, threatening to send it flying off the desktop. She put down the quill pen and reached for the gold chain hanging about her neck. Her father's heavy seal ring, hers now, nestled between her breasts. Because it was too large to fit her fingers, even her thumb, she wore it as a necklace. She pulled the heavy chain over her head and set it and the ring upon the ink-blotched but mostly blank page. She sighed. Assuming she decided to send it, the missive would have to be recopied. There was no help for it. Now that the wheels of her abduction scheme were in motion, she couldn't seem to organize her thoughts.

If the trio of warriors she'd dispatched the night before had succeeded in their mission, Ewan Fraser would be warming her bed ere nightfall.

The thought sent her heart hitching and her limbs trembling as though she were a child once more, testing her courage by climbing atop the parapet wall and dangling her wobbly legs over the side. Forcing her gaze to the straight drop below, she'd imagined the rock-strewn cliffs as a dragon's sharp-toothed jaws, a great gobbling beastie waiting to snatch her up should she misstep and fall.

A decade later, she felt as though she were about to plunge headfirst into a different sort of abyss, one ruled by recrimination and revenge.

Tensions between the MacLeods and the Frasers had run high over the years, cattle thieving and poaching the whiskey stills being the chief complaints lobbed by both sides. But then three months ago, Ewan's twin, Callum, had murdered Brianna's husband, Donald, in cold blood. She and Donald had hardly been a love match, but they had grown up together. Though she'd only married him out of duty, and hard duty it had been, she surely hadn't wished him dead.

On the surface Donald had possessed a disposition as affable as his sunshine-gold hair and mild hazel eyes. But once they'd wed, he'd revealed a strong stubborn streak. Ignoring her pleas and her father's command, he'd taken it upon himself to meet with Callum Fraser in the hope that the accusations of stealing might be put to rest once and for all. When he hadn't returned by nightfall, a search party was dispatched. Guided by torchlight and the beacon of a perfect full moon, they'd found his body by the loch, a bloodied rock lying scarce a foot away from his caved-in skull, the scrap of Fraser plaid in his stiffened fist the final damning evidence.

The shock had caused Brianna to miscarry their babe. The loss of her child was not one she could easily forgive. Because of the close blood bond between brothers, she had every right to extract payment from Ewan for the harm his sibling had done. Still, the necessity of setting aside that happy fair day memory struck her as yet another loss to be mourned.

But she had no choice. Her father lay in the kirkyard these two days past, his big body shrunken by illness and wrapped in winding sheets dampened by Brianna's tears. With his dying breath, he'd entrusted the MacLeod clan, lands and stronghold to her safekeeping. Already there were rumblings among her advisors, the "old gentlemen," that no mere woman, not even a favored daughter, could possibly serve in his stead. Surely their enemy, the Frasers, would see a female chieftain as an invitation to attack. Though the castle might be as stalwart a fortress as any ever built, there was the safety of the crofters and others living beyond the protection of its walls to consider. A healthy bairn with equal parts MacLeod and Fraser blood would end the feud far better than any treaty written on parchment or sealed with a handshake and a dram.

She needed Ewan Fraser as she'd hoped to never again need another man.

A high-pitched wailing had her looking back over her

shoulder to the bed. Milread, her childhood nurse, stood waving a willow branch over the turned-down coverlet. The old woman chanted some nonsense about a one-eyed snake emerging triumphant after burrowing in a warm, receptive hole. Widow though she was, the frank image had Brianna blushing.

"Milread, I'm warning you, if you scatter so much as one rose petal over those sheets, I'll have you whipped within an inch of your life." She stabbed the tip of the pen back in the ink pot and sent up a silent prayer to the saints to grant her the patience to see her through to the end of this day.

Cackling, Milread dropped the branch and shuffled to Brianna's side. "Nay, sweeting, you willna. You love me too well to beat me, and I'm too old for it anyhow."

Brianna shook her head, torn between weariness and amusement. "Forgive me, Milread. I'd no cause to speak to you so sharply." Since Brianna's mother's death, the old woman had acted more as parent than servant.

Milread tucked a stray strand of red-gold hair behind her former charge's ear. "Nay matter, poppet. It must feel as though you're carrying the weight of the world on your slender shoulders, but dinna fret. The night your dear da died, I read the runes on your behalf. The stones foretell of a long and happy life with one bairn soon on its way and a lusty raven-haired husband to fill your belly with plenty more in the years to come."

As tempting as it was to believe her future might be so neatly settled, Brianna was skeptical. Though Milread put great stock in the ancient form of prophecy, Brianna didn't know how a bagful of cold carved stones could divine such details as her future "husband's" hair color and sexual stamina. Most likely Milread had once heard the Fraser twins described as dark-haired and light-eyed, and pushed the information to the back of her mind until now. As for the lusty part, well, it was certainly a lovely thought.

"You should eat something." Milread's nagging brought her back to the present. "You'll need your strength for your bridegroom when he arrives." The wise woman jerked her chin to the canopied bed, the twig lying in the center.

"Ewan Fraser is not my bridegroom," Brianna snapped. Her soon-to-be sexual liaison with the brother of her sworn enemy was a tender topic for any number of reasons. Softening, she added, "I've no plan to wed again. And even if I did, it wouldn't be to the twin of my husband's murderer."

Milread shifted her crooked shoulders. "'Tis only the Lord's plans that go unchallenged, milady. Mortal men and women must accept what Providence decrees. A marriage will heal the rift between the clans whether there is issue or not. In time, it might also heal milady's heart."

Brianna let out a mirthless laugh. "I no longer have a heart, so there is naught to heal." With the losses mounting, it was prudent not to feel.

Milread fixed her cloudy gaze on Brianna's face. Though half-blind, the wise woman saw more than most fully sighted people did. "Three months is a long time for a lass to bed alone, and Lord Donald was far from lusty."

Heat hit Brianna's face, for it was no more than the truth. Donald hadn't been "bold and buxom" in their bedchamber despite his marriage vow. Even if he'd shown more vigor, Brianna's head had been clouded with foolish fancies of blood oaths and stolen kisses, raven-colored locks that felt like feathers and clear gray eyes that seemed to see straight through to her soul.

Milread's tender gaze fell on her face. "It wasna your fault, wean. With the right man in your bed, it's a passionate lassie you'll be."

Once again the old woman had all but read Brianna's mind. Feeling a trickle of tears on her cheek, Brianna quickly looked away. The bald truth was her husband hadn't desired her. With every shunning, she had felt a piece of her soul splinter and die.

"I'll be five and twenty on my next saint's day, so I'm no lassie. As for Ewan Fraser, all I want from him is his seed in my belly. Once I have that, he can go back to his kinsmen, or to the devil, for all I care."

To his kinsmen or the devil. Since it was a devil's bargain she was about to make, the sentiment seemed fitting.

A rap outside the chamber door had both women whipping about. Nerves drawn taut as a bowstring, Brianna gave the call to enter.

The door opened, revealing the barrel-chested form of her father's cousin, Duncan. Father to the warrior Hugh, he had served as her father's privy councillor for decades. Entering his sixtieth year, he still stood broad-shouldered and lance-straight.

One arm banded in mourning black, he touched his silvered forelock and scraped a low bow. "The Fraser prisoner awaits your pleasure, milady."

Hearing that her plan had succeeded, that Ewan Fraser was indeed a captive within her castle, sent the enormity of what she'd done crashing down upon Brianna like a rock slide. She opened her mouth to answer, but her tongue felt stiff and stuck.

"Shall I bring him to you before the court commences?" Duncan prompted.

The court! Saints preserve her, she'd been so caught up in contemplating Ewan's arrival that she'd as good as forgotten her obligation.

According to custom, the laird collected the rents on quarter days as well as held court for his—or in her case, *her*—people. Petitioners had begun arriving the night before, bedding down in the great hall and vestibule to wait for the chance to have their grievances heard and their wrongs redressed. Bringing an outsider, a prisoner in chains no less, into the session would never do. She glanced down at the half-finished letter and decided to leave it unsent for the present. For now, the fewer who knew of her intentions, the better. With luck, by the time Callum Fraser discovered the whereabouts of his twin, Brianna's end would have been met, and Ewan would be on his way back home.

She shook her head. "Nay, hold him till the last case is resolved and the court dismissed. Then bring him to me privately…in my, uh…chamber."

The retainer hesitated, and Brianna felt a telltale warmth trickling into her face and throat.

"As you wish, milady." As he rose, his gaze alighted on the paper lying on the desk. "A ransom note to be delivered to the Fraser, milady? Shall I arrange for a messenger to see to its dispatch?"

Brianna hesitated, his presumption stirring a vague annoyance. "I shall hold off on sending it for the time being, but thank you." Uncomfortable with his scrutiny, she opened the desk drawer and slipped the letter inside.

He nodded and then began backing toward the door. As he did, a sunbeam slashing through the window glass found its way to his weathered face, revealing a kaleidoscope of bruising.

Brianna asked, "Duncan, is that a black eye I see?"

Jaw tight, he nodded. "The prisoner was less than… cooperative."

Remembering Ewan as a lean, lanky boy more likely to raise his flute than his fists, Brianna was puzzled. Graybeard though he was, Duncan was still a warrior with whom to be reckoned, broad of build and well able to wield his claymore with strength and skill.

"I see." Rather than cause him further embarrassment, she gestured toward the door. "I shall see you below anon."

He bowed. "As you will, milady."

Brianna waited for him to leave. Once he had, she pushed back her chair and rose.

Silent until now, Milread leaned over Brianna and tapped a long yellowed fingernail on the desktop. "Dinna leave your ring lying about, milady. The laird's seal isna safe anywhere but on your person."

Grateful for the reminder, Brianna picked up the ring, dropped the chain over her head and returned the ring to its resting place. If she decided to send the ransom

letter, she would seal it—and all their fates—by pressing
the carved cornelian stone bearing the MacLeod motto,
Hold Fast, and bull motif into the warm wax.

"Thank you, Milread. It seems I am not myself this
day."

"Whisht, if not yourself, then who is it you think to
be? Take heart, milady. Your da schooled you well. You
already ken what it means to be a laird. 'Tis time to go
forth and be a woman."

"HEAR YE, HEAR YE ALL, The MacLeod's court is now
in session…."

Brianna looked down from her carved wooden dais to
the packed great hall. The trestle tables and long backless
benches had been pushed against the walls to accommodate the crowd, the standing men, women and children
stacked like cordwood on either side of the wide center
aisle. Though she had attended many a court day over the
years, this time felt very different. This time she was
laird. Every eye in the room was riveted in her direction.
More curious gazes rained down upon her from the railed
minstrel's gallery above. She could almost fancy that
Malcolm, the first MacLeod chief, peered over her
shoulder from the tapestry on the wall at her back, mea-
suring her worth, her readiness—her heart.

She passed the next few hours listening to the peti-
tions brought before her—lords seeking land grants and
other favors from the new laird, disputes over property
boundaries and one adultery case in which the wronged
wife had slit her wayward husband's nose whilst he
slept. No matter how large or trifling the complaint,

Brianna made it a point to grant all parties their say before rendering her decision.

She used the time between cases to sketch several mental pictures of a mature Ewan Fraser. Undoubtedly, his face and form had filled out with the years, but she wanted to believe his eyes retained the crystal clarity of her memory. Truth be told, she was every whit as nervous as a bride on her wedding eve, far more so than she'd been on that momentous occasion itself. Unseemly as it was, she couldn't wait to find herself alone in bed with her enemy. And yet her eagerness was tainted with a hefty dose of self-doubt. Ten years ago he'd called her pretty, but ten years was a long time. Who knew whether or not he'd find her pleasing now? He would, however, find her clean. She'd tended to her teeth that morning with a hazel twig, as was her custom, and then scrubbed them for longer than usual with a cloth dipped in tooth powder of sage and salt until they shone like polished marble. Before coming below, she'd sweetened her breath with the fennel and rosemary vinegar rinse that was Milread's special concoction. Still, Brianna wondered if it was enough. And then there was her hair, a disaster since birth. The wavy, fire-red tresses had a canny knack for finding their way free of any style. Earlier, she'd tried experimenting, then given up and plaited it in her customary braid.

The banging of her steward's gavel announced they'd moved on to the next case, a dispute involving two women laying claim to the same bairn, a bonny boy with golden curls, a cherub's chubby cheeks and the most perfect baby fingers Brianna had ever beheld. Gazing at the child, struggling in the older woman's awkward embrace, she felt a desperate emptiness wash over her. She needed a baby to end the blood feud and solidify her position as laird. But beyond those practical purposes, she so very badly wanted to be a mother.

She dealt herself a brisk mental shake and divided her gaze between the two women standing before her. The younger looked to be scarcely older than sixteen, and wore a threadbare gown of bright yellow, the harlot's shade. Brianna felt a stab of sympathy. Dark crescents banded the girl's tear-bright blue eyes. Her stick-thin arms hung slack at her sides as though, bereft of a baby to hold, she wasn't sure what to do with them. Despite her lowly status, her pale gold hair was elaborately braided and her bare feet and ankles scrubbed clean. In the midst of her distress, she must have stopped at the bathing font in the alcove before entering.

Brianna shifted her gaze back to the other woman. Older than her rival by a good five years, she was the very picture of propriety. A wimple covered her head and neck so that not a single strand of hair peeked out. With her unnaturally high forehead knitted in a frown, she held the bairn as though he were a sack of meal rather than her own flesh and blood.

The blonde dropped to her knees. "My laird, I pray you will hear my petition, for you are my last hope. A fortnight ago, this woman entered my hovel in the wee hours and stole my Alasdair."

The woman holding the child stomped forward. Above the bairn's bawling, she shouted, "All lies, my laird. This is my own sweet Fearghas, the light of my

life and the spitting image of his dear departed da. Surely you wouldna accept the word of a common slut over mine?"

Brianna took an instant dislike to the widow, but in fairness resolved to hear both sides. "Let her finish, madam. Your turn to speak will come soon enough." She nodded for the kneeling girl to continue.

The young woman drew a gulping breath. "I was just finishing feeding Alasdair his supper—he's just started to take some porridge along with my milk, but he'll only stomach it if it's laced with plenty of honey and cream—when she burst through our door and wrenched my baby from my arms. I gave chase, but the night watchman held me back and took her part because she is a burgher's widow, while I am…but a whore." The confession broke off on a sob.

The unsparing admission tore at Brianna's heart. "I see." She turned to the widow. "And you, madam, what have you to say?"

Eyes hard as stones, she shrugged. "The bitch lies. The bairn is my son, my one and only, and all I have left to comfort me in my grief. Being a widow yourself, milady, I know you will take my part."

Brianna didn't care for the woman's manipulative manner. "This is a court of law, madam. We deal in truth here, not sentiment. Have you any documents, a baptismal record or the like, to bear you out?"

The widow hesitated, her sly gaze sliding away to the benches lining the far wall. "Nay, there was a mishap, a terrible fire. The parish records were destroyed. It was all verra tragic." Brianna hadn't heard of any fire, but for the present she let the remark pass. "I do have a witness to the birth, though." She speared a spiny finger toward the seated audience. "Yonder godly monk will bear me out."

She shoved the baby into the arms of a nearby guard and vaulted from the petitioner's box toward the benches. With his tonsured head pillowed against the cornerstone, the monk slept, his snores reaching the dais.

Tugging the sleeve of his brown cassock, she shrilled, "Brother Bartholomew, awake and tell them how you saw me birth this bairn with your own two eyes." Holding on with both hands, she yanked him to his feet.

Blinking, he turned his fleshy face toward Brianna. "Aye, 'tis so. I was present for the birth."

Brianna doubted it. "A man of God attending a lady's lying-in seems verra odd to me."

He answered with a vigorous nod, his double chins wobbling like a pudding. "I have some skills in animal husbandry, and as there was no midwife at hand, I did what I might."

Striving to keep a sober face, Brianna nodded. "I see. Very noble of you, good brother, and a fine job you made of it, too. A brawer, bonnier bairn I've never before seen."

She glanced at the two women. The burgher's widow stared blankly back, but the pretty young woman in the whore's dress glowed with pride.

Brianna was no Solomon, but it was clear to her which of the women was the child's true mother. As laird, her word was law, but she could hardly order the boy split in half like a melon—or could she?

Hoping the spirit of the ancient king's wisdom might

serve the cause of present-day justice, she addressed the two petitioners. "You must share him."

"Share him?" The widow's thin brows shot up to her plucked hairline.

Brianna nodded. "Aye, for the first fortnight of each month he will bide with you, widow." She shifted her gaze to the young mother still on her knees. "And for the final fortnight he will bide with you, lady. The first woman who fails to hand him over at the appointed time will forfeit her right to him altogether."

The widow blew out a breath and then shrugged. "It sounds a bit daft, but I suppose half a loaf is better than none."

Addressing the young mother, Brianna gentled her tone and asked, "And what say you to this arrangement, lass?"

The girl slowly rose, as though she'd gained several decades in the past few minutes. She sent a look of raw yearning toward the child. Struggling against the burly guard's hold, he stretched out chubby baby arms for her to take him.

Eyes streaming, she faced Brianna and shook her head. "I am afraid my answer must be no, milady."

As caught up in the enfolding drama as any onlooker, Brianna released her bated breath. "Are you certain? Mind, the answer you give here today must stand for all the long, lonesome years to come."

Her expression bleak, the girl nodded. "Aye, I mind it well enough. But a child raised by two mothers canna help but come into manhood like a sapling buffeted by two opposing winds. He would be forever torn for want of knowing where he belongs and who he is. As I am his mother who bore him and who loves him more than my own life, I canna condemn him to such a fate to serve my own selfishness."

Touched by the display of maternal love and wisdom in one so young, Brianna felt tears pressing the backs of her eyes. "Lass, your simple, heartfelt words and selfless love have proved beyond all doubt that the bairn is yours." She shifted her gaze to the widow, who seemed to shrink into the wainscoting. "If ever you show your sour face in my court again, madam, rest assured I shall see you sent to my scullery for a very long and very unpleasant lesson in humility—*after* I have your lying tongue cut from your head. Now take your false priest and your false words and leave before I change my mind about forgoing the pleasure."

The widow didn't dally. Her eyes wide as saucers, she hiked up her skirts, turned tail and ran toward the door as quickly as her pointed slippers would take her, the plump monk bringing up the rear.

Beaming, the young mother whirled back to Brianna. "Oh, thank you, milady. Thank you."

She ran up to the guard, who handed over the baby with a smile. Wee Alasdair stopped crying the instant his mother's slender arms wrapped about him. With a sigh, he nestled his flushed face against her shoulder and snuggled in to sleep.

Brianna swallowed against the lump in her throat. Stepping into her father's shoes was no small feat, but moments such as this brought their own reward, a sense of soul-deep satisfaction more priceless than any family jewels.

The girl bobbed a clumsy curtsy. Shifting the baby to her hip, she turned and started up the aisle.

Brianna tamped down her smile and adopted a solemn expression befitting a laird. "Halt, lady. We are not yet finished our business."

She stopped and turned about. Smile dimming, she asked, "Milady?"

"You have not yet told me your name."

The girl hesitated and nibbled her lower lip. "I am called Alys, milady."

"Well, Alys, you and the bairn still require food on your table and a roof over your heads. Without a husband, how do you mean to provide for your son?"

Alys's slender shoulders drooped. Hugging her sleeping child close, as if he might be snatched from her yet again, she shook her head. "I am young yet and passably pretty, or so I am told. Men seem to fancy me. To keep my baby fed and clothed, I can bear the touch of strangers if I must. For Alasdair, I can bear anything."

"Could you bear tending the kitchen garden and learning to work in the stillroom, and mayhap on occasion helping my old nurse with drying and pressing her healing herbs?"

Alys's blue eyes widened. Her rosebud mouth fell open. "Milady?"

Brianna nodded. "In a castle the size of this, there is always need for another pair of helping hands. What say you?"

Beside her, Duncan bent and whispered into her ear, "Bringing a fallen woman and her bastard into the castle—are you sure that is wise, milady?"

Brianna turned her face up to his. Reminding herself that though he was old enough to be her da, she was his laird and he her servant, she dropped her voice and answered, "My father was ever ready to render aid to those willing to work to alter their lives for the better. I cannot say for certain if he would approve of my decision, but I like to think he would. Regardless, I am laird now. As such, I must trust in the truth as recognized by my own eyes and mind—and heart." Turning to address her steward in a voice meant to carry out over the court, she said, "See that this woman and her child are quartered above the buttery. Tomorrow will be soon enough to instruct her in her duties. For the night, I venture she and the bairn will benefit greatly from a hearty meal and a sound sleep."

"Oh, thank you, milady. Thank you. You willna be sorry, I swear it."

Humbled by the girl's worshipful gaze, Brianna smiled and waved her off to the steward. Turning back to Duncan, she asked, "What is the next case to be heard?"

Jaw tight, he shook his head. "That was the last of the petitioners, milady."

Brianna's heart kicked into a canter. With no more cases to be heard, she was free to retire to her chamber—and Ewan Fraser. "In that case, you have my permission to dismiss—"

"God's blood, woman, what the devil do you think you're about?"

Heads swiveled to the rear of the room, where a braw, if bruised and bloodied, dark-haired man draped in torn Fraser tartan glared at Brianna with crystalline gray eyes.

3

"HALT, KNAVE!"

Rather than heed the pursuing guard's panting cry, Ewan Fraser strode down the aisle between the benches, his chains striking sparks off the slate floor, his gaze trained on the startled face of the hall's chief occupant: The MacLeod, Brianna MacLeod—Brie. What twisted turn of Fate had transformed his youth's sweetest memory into his present-day nemesis, his curse?

Three of her men had set upon him that morning whilst he slept wrapped in his plaid beside the banked campfire. In the hours since, he'd lost track of the thrashings, the episodes melding into one stinking sinkhole of pain. He'd been fisted in the face so many times he couldn't tell if his nose was broken, but he was fairly certain one or more of his bottom teeth were knocked loose. The latter struck him as ironic, for until that morning he'd managed to reach the age of two and twenty with a full set. His left eye was swollen shut, his vision hazy. Squinting, he recognized the grizzled warrior at Brianna's side as the leader of her merry band of marauders. The graybeard had taken great delight in flogging him with a horse whip after the two young warriors bound his arms. Who would have supposed an old man would be the one to give him his first fight scars? Saint Michael, the patron saint of warriors, must be having a hearty laugh at his expense.

He came to the velvet rope cordoning off the dais just as a wave of dizziness washed over him. From behind, a heavy foot struck out, catching the back of his right knee and dropping him to the floor.

The old warrior on the platform lanced him a wintry look. "Ewan Fraser, milady, younger brother of the clan chief. The prisoner awaits your pleasure."

A collective gasp ricocheted from the hall's high ceiling and sturdy stone walls. Murmuring voices repeated his name again and again, the words echoing inside his throbbing skull, keeping pace with the pounding.

Ewan...Fraser, Fraser, Fraser...

A velvety voice rose above the sound of blood rushing in his ears. "My *pleasure,* as I recall it, was that he wasna to be harmed, nay so much as a single hair on his head. And yet he looks as though he's been used as a battering ram. What is the meaning of defying my order and bringing him to me thus?"

She was defending him! Improbably, Ewan felt his heart swelling and his spirits lifting. He forced himself back to sanity, reminding himself that his would-be champion was the same soulless witch who'd ordered him abducted.

"Well said, milady." A boot in his back kept him from rising, but he clapped his hands, steeling himself to ignore his swollen knuckles and the manacles rubbing the flesh from his wrists. "What is the meaning indeed?"

He knew he was likely a fool to speak out, but at this point what was one more pummeling? "I am brought here as a captive, abducted from my clan lands, though I've offered no insult and committed no wrong."

Gasps traveled the chamber's four corners. Brianna rose and descended the carpet-covered steps, stopping on the landing above him.

His nose must not be broken, for he scented her fresh springtime fragrance, an olfactory memory from all those many years ago. Cherry blossom mixed with some familiar flowering herb he was hard-pressed to name, but suddenly wanted very badly to taste.

Looking down on him, she said, "You have far too bold a tongue for a prisoner."

Ewan hoisted his hammering head—and promptly lost his breath. His throat dry as sawdust, he moistened his parched lips. "And you, lady, have far too fair a face for a laird."

It was no more than the truth. Fox fire–green eyes fringed with thick smoke-colored lashes raked over him. Viewed up close, he confirmed, her complexion was too creamy to come from a jar of leaden paste, her high forehead owed nothing to the current fashion for plucking, and her full, bee-stung lips were fashioned more for kissing than pouting. A thin scarf of white linen banded with a gold cord fluttered over her copper-colored hair, the long tresses gathered into a single waist-length plait nearly as thick as his upper arm.

Imagining himself wrapping the skein of fiery hair about his hand and reeling her toward him until their lips met and their bodies melded, he felt his cock come to life. Heavy and hard and aching, it was the one part of him still able to function without pain. He lowered his bound hands to conceal his crotch. At the same time, he took another leap into danger and slid his gaze over her body. The pretty plump girl of his memory had become a lovely, lithe woman. She stood tall, almost as tall as he. Her simple outer gown was plain green. Its loose fit hinted at strong, slender arms, a pleasingly full bosom and a narrow waist. A kirtle cinched about the latter, holding a massive ring of keys. He wondered if it held the means to his freedom. He suspected it did.

The clearing of a throat snapped him back to the present. "Scriptural law proclaims an eye for an eye and a tooth for a tooth." She was addressing him and her gaze was cold as snow. "Because of your brother, my husband and babe both lay in the kirkyard. Your brother, Callum, owes me a life, Ewan Fraser, *two* lives to be exact, and I mean to collect payment on the debt through you."

"My brother had no hand in your lord's death. I swear it upon mine honor."

In the midst of vouchsafing Callum's innocence, Ewan found the significance of her statement striking him like yet another fist to the gut. God's blood, she meant to murder him! Until now he'd assumed she would hold him prisoner and then ransom him back to his brother, but not so, it seemed. Panic slammed into him, the force exceeding any physical blow he'd so far received.

Scenes from his past twenty-two years skittered through his thoughts. He found himself regretting no deed in particular, but rather the many deeds he'd now never have the chance to do. Travel the world. Teach his future son to fish. Give Brianna MacLeod a proper kiss. After the clumsy embrace they'd shared as children, he'd spent years hoping for the opportunity to do better by her. Who knew how long he had before she sent him off to meet his maker? But for certain, traveling and procreating would never happen for him now. Looking up into her cool gaze and composed face, it occurred to him that one final wish might yet be fulfilled.

"Your honor, indeed," she scoffed. "Fraser honor holds no worth in this hall, sir."

"In that case, lady, I commit myself to your *tender* mercy. I only ask that you grant me a warrior's death and have the big one over there—" he gestured to the graybeard towering behind her "—strike my head from my shoulders with a claymore or a sword as befits my station." After all he'd suffered, subjecting him to disemboweling or burning at the stake hardly seemed sporting.

"Strike off your head?" Her green eyes popped and the luscious lips he contemplated kissing fell open as though making way for his tongue.

Ignoring the hammering inside his skull—he'd be past all fleshly feeling soon enough—he nodded. "Aye, but before you see the deed done, I crave a boon. One kiss from milady's honeyed lips and then I'll greet Saint Peter with a hearty hey ho."

The corners of her full mouth twitched, the closest she'd so far come to a smile. "You're a knave, Ewan Fraser, and like as not you deserve to be drawn and quartered in payment for all the maidenly hearts you've broken."

Drawn and quartered—dear God, what a bloodthirsty wench she was. He'd best make the kiss a good one, lingering and deep, whilst he still had the full complement of his manly parts. "First let us have that kiss, milady."

He started up from his knees to claim it. Head swimming, he struggled to find his footing on the stone flagging. Before he could, the chamber dipped and swayed, the floor falling in beneath him. Stars poked through the encroaching blackness, performing a dizzy dance before his burning eyes.

Watching her prisoner fall over onto his side, Brianna could scarcely credit the proof of her eyes. Ewan Fraser, bold warrior, had fainted. Dark hair plastered his damp forehead and his handsome face looked flushed, whether from fever or temper or both she couldn't say. One powerful arm locked about his torso. The protective posture stretched the soiled saffron shirt across his broad shoulders and back, revealing the whip marks bleeding through the torn cloth. Whip marks!

Fury lanced through her. She swung about to Duncan, who'd followed her to the edge of the steps.

Aware of the petitioners watching goggle-eyed from the benches, as though a passion play was in progress, she dropped her voice and hissed, "I told you he was not to be harmed."

She might have had him abducted to serve a greater good, but she was no torturer. Once her end was achieved, she meant to return him to his kinsman hale and whole. Hurting him had never been a part of her plan. Still, badly beaten though he was, at least they wouldn't have to call in the bonesetter. Bruises and scrapes and torn flesh would heal with time, but more often than not, a broken bone meant lifelong laming.

Duncan bowed his grizzled head. "I have failed you, milady, and yet I canna say how I could have brought him to you any other way. Fraser or not, a bolder, braver warrior I have never before faced."

She swiveled to Duncan's son, Hugh. The young warrior had been charged with guarding Ewan and keeping him out of sight until the court was dismissed. Bruises rimmed his one eye and his stance was markedly hunched.

Voice still lowered, she said, "And you were to have kept him away from the court."

"And so I would have, milady, only he…"

The smooth-shaven faced flushed, and Brianna prompted, "He what?"

"He kneed me in the, uh…ballocks." Darting a look in Duncan's direction, he added, "My father speaks true, milady. The Fraser's stubbornness causes him to come to you thus. He fought like Satan's own. Earlier today it took the three of us to subdue him, and even then he wouldn't leave off his fashing."

Three warriors had been charged with abducting him, and Ewan had come close to besting them all. Brianna felt her chest tightening with ill-placed pride and some other emotion she had yet to name. Face flushing, she returned her gaze to the fallen man. It was too late to undo the clumsy capture, but from here on, she meant to see Ewan made as comfortable and treated as civilly as circumstances would allow, even if it meant tending him with her own hands. The latter thought sent a starburst-like thrill shooting through her.

As if he sensed her nearness, his closed eyelids fluttered. He blinked and returned to consciousness. His left eye was swollen shut, but his right appeared unharmed. The moonstone-pale orb pierced hers, stealing her breath and muddling her thoughts.

"Sweet Brie, whatever befell the braw, bonny lassie who was to have been my bride?" His voice trailed off, his eyes rolling back in his head and his body slackening.

So he remembered their betrothal pact. An invisible knot cinched Brianna's throat. Tender emotions she thought to have locked away with his flute flooded her. Their fair-day meeting must have meant something to him, too.

She started toward him, but Duncan's hand found her elbow. "He speaks in riddles, milady. With your permission, I will see him removed to the dungeon until he is well enough to be brought to you."

Brianna shrugged free of his hold. "You will do no such thing. Lord Ewan is not a common criminal but a noble hostage. He doesna belong in a dungeon cell but in a chamber befitting his rank and station. Have him carried to the laird's chamber, *my* chamber, and mind this time your men do my bidding with a gentle hand."

An hour later, Brianna strode down the rush-lit corridor to the laird's chamber, a chalice in one hand and a taper in the other. Looped over her wrist was the basket filled with Milread's special salve. After dismissing the court, she'd sent her old nursemaid to minister to Ewan's needs, including bathing. Mention of willow twigs, rose petals or true love was strictly forbidden.

Her steps slowed as she approached the bedchamber.

For the past ten years, she'd carried about the memory of Ewan Fraser as a lanky boy with crystal clear eyes and a good-natured grin. The eyes hadn't changed a whit, but everything else about him had altered mightily. The Ewan Fraser waiting for her within was very much a man, and a braw, beautiful one at that. A braw beautiful man she would soon bed, assuming the thrashing they'd dealt him hadn't rendered him incapable.

A guard stood outside her door. She recognized him as Seamus, known as the broken man. The young warrior was without kith or kin, though Duncan swore he was one of his most trustworthy guards and able fighters. Still, his long, pointed chin, narrow darting gaze and scar-puckered cheek reminded her of a rat.

Seamus bowed. "Good eve, milady. Lord Duncan bade me stand watch over the prisoner and…you."

Ewan's barging into her great hall while her court was in session had wrought havoc with her intention to keep him quietly confined until her plan bore…*fruit*. By now the whole castle must know that he'd been brought to her private rooms.

Glad of the early-evening shadows to mask the heat that must be branding her cheeks, she nodded. "So I see."

"Sleep well, milady." He held the door for her, his gaze brushing over her and his mouth twisting into a smirk.

Telling herself guilt must be making her imagine things, she stepped inside and drew the door closed behind her. Shadows engulfed her, relieved only by the flickering of the fire set in the grate and a brace of candles mounted in wall brackets. Her gaze swung to the bed— and the dark form lying chained in the center. *Ah, Ewan…*

Iron manacles banded his wrists, the carved bolsters serving as anchors for the heavy chains that drew his powerful arms high over his head. Seeing him thus, she felt her heart lurch, her regret as piercing as any physical pain. If only they'd been free to fulfill their fair-day vow, they might have come together as man and wife with open arms and free wills and joyous hearts instead of this travesty of a union forged of regret and revenge.

She walked up to the chest at the foot of the bed and paused. Shadowed though the room was, she fancied she felt Ewan tracking her movements with his eyes. She'd ordered him stripped and bathed for the practical purpose of caring for his wounds. Until now, she hadn't given much thought to how she would feel about putting her own less-than-perfect body on display. Tall, full-breasted and full-hipped, she wasn't the plump, pretty child who once had fit so neatly against Ewan's lean, boyish form.

But they weren't children anymore or lovers or even friends. A wave of sadness struck her. Steeling herself to ignore it, she set the candle down atop the desk along with the basket and chalice. Reaching up, she removed her veiled headdress. Beneath it, her hair was gathered into a single long braid. She had the fleeting thought she ought to comb her fingers through the waves and leave it loose as she had on her wedding night, but decided against doing so. Drawing any parallel to that ill-fated night would seem like a portent of doom.

Instead, she unpinned her plaid. She unwound the length of wool and laid it aside, along with the broach that bore her clan crest, a bull's horns and the motto

Hold Fast in Latin. She cast another glance upward to the bed. He hadn't stirred. Mayhap he truly was asleep. Fingers clumsy, she unfastened her sleeves and then unlaced the front of her gown; the latter she pulled over her head. Modesty had her stopping at her shift. The fine linen whispered just above her ankles. She took off the chain with the seal ring, too, and put it in the drawer. Making a mental note to remember to put it back on later, she folded her clothes and set them in a neat stack on the chair seat. By the time she'd finished, her hands were clammy and shaking.

She retrieved the chalice and basket and rounded to the side of the bed. Leaning over, she whispered, "Ewan, do you sleep?"

His eyes were closed. Long lashes shadowed his high cheekbones. Either the brutal handling had worn him out or he was pretending, for he didn't so much as blink. Skin heating, she skimmed her gaze over his body, naked except for a swathe of linen thrown over his thighs. Even blanketed by cuts and bruises and angry red welts, he was impossibly beautiful. Broad of shoulder and lean of waist and hip, his pale skin stretched taut over sinewy muscle and long bones, he brought to mind a statue carved in marble or alabaster. Only Ewan was no cold tomb statue, but a living, breathing man.

She drew back, a foreign throbbing settling between her thighs. At least one order of hers had been obeyed. He was clean. His damp skin smelled of Milread's rosemary mint soap, as well as some other scent that was his alone, like the smell of air just after a cleansing springtime shower. The old woman had washed his hair, as well. The pillow beneath his head was damp and the dark tresses shone like polished ebony. One damp lock fell over his forehead and over his swollen, shut eye. Overcome by a sudden tenderness, Brianna reached to brush it back.

Ewan snapped open his good eye and glared up at her. "Come to gloat, milady?"

She jumped back, dripping tallow onto the bedcovers. "You startled me."

"Really?" The black brow framing his good eye arched upward. "You'll pardon me if I find that a wee bit difficult to fathom."

In the thrall of his moonstone gaze, Brianna felt the breath lock inside her lungs. Even masked in bruises, his lean face was a masterpiece of male beauty. She ran her gaze over his high brow, molded aquiline nose and firm, full mouth—the very same mouth that had gifted her with her first real kiss all those many years ago— and felt a spurt of sticky warmth trickle down her leg.

Embarrassed by her body's response, she set the basket down and held out the cup. "I've brought you something." She hesitated and then settled next to him, her hip brushing his side.

He pressed his lips together and cut a wary glance to the cup. "What is it?"

"Caudle." Reading the question in his eyes, she elaborated, "Mulled wine with bits of brown bread, sugar, eggs and spices to render it flavorful. It is an English recipe. My old nurse taught me to make it. It will ease and nourish you."

"Poison me, more like." He clamped together his

swollen lips, beautiful all the same, and shook his dark head. "I'll no drink so much as one drop. If you mean to murder me, then do the deed out in the open as a laird would. Poison is the weapon of cowards—and women." His disdainful expression conveyed he considered the two to be cut from the same cloth.

Leaning over him, Brianna found herself fighting the urge to laugh. She slid her arm beneath his neck and shoulders to raise him, and pressed the rim of the cup to his swollen lips. "If I wanted you dead, Ewan Fraser, you'd be dead ere now. So drink."

In the end, hunger and thirst took precedence over pride. He drank, gingerly at first but then with great greedy gulps. Brianna felt a stab of guilt, but tamped it down by reminding herself that, fair-day memories aside, Ewan Fraser was still her enemy. His brother's crime made him so and they not only shared the same blood, but, as twins, had bided together in their mother's womb. Beyond the necessities of shelter and sustenance, he didn't deserve her consideration.

She eased his head down on the pillow, and then set the empty cup aside and reached for the basket. Though his upper body was immobile, his gaze followed her every move. She brought out the jar of Milread's special salve.

Twisting off the top, Brianna warned, "This might sting a wee bit, but mostly it should soothe."

"What is it?"

"It's no poison if that's what you're worried for." She dipped in two fingers and then held them up to show him. "There's yarrow, red clover, yellow wood sorrel and other ingredients that aid in flesh mending."

He sniffed, one dark brow lifting again. "Don't tell me you're a healer, too?"

She shook her head. Keeping her touch light, she started on his shoulders. "What little I know of herbs and such my old nurse taught me. Her remedies include everything from amulets to remove evil eye curses to love potions…for silly young maids," she added, not wanting him to think she'd ever sought out such nonsense.

"Love potions?" He eyed her with open skepticism. "Are there any in that wee basket?"

Heat hit Brianna's cheeks. She shook her head. "Nay, I wouldna wish the curse of being in love on my worst enemy."

He shrugged and then winced as though the movement caused him pain. "What would you wish on me then?" Not giving her opportunity to answer, he added, "If it's ransom that you seek, you should know my brother would just as soon see my head on a pike as part with his coin."

Gathering her thoughts, she capped the jar, dropped it back inside the basket and set the latter aside. Lifting her gaze, she said, "It's not ransom I seek but peace— and a baby. A child with both our bloods will heal the hatred between our clans more so than any treaty. That, Ewan Fraser, is why I've brought you here."

Even with shadows dappling his face, there was no missing the shock pulling at his features. "You had me kidnapped so that I might service you as a stud would a mare in heat? You must be mad, milady."

Was the idea of bedding her truly that loathsome to him? Shame scored Brianna's face, the heat bleeding into her hairline. Duty alone kept her from fleeing the room.

Rather than look away, she forced her eyes to meet his. "And yet earlier in the great hall you claimed a kiss as your last earthly request."

His gaze settled on her mouth. Brianna felt as though she were shrinking, but steeled herself not to show it. She had always been self-conscious of her mouth. Too wide and full-lipped for fashion, it was her very worst feature.

"Aye, I did."

Enemy or not, she felt herself softening toward him. "Do you want to kiss me now?" God knew she very much wanted to kiss him.

There was just enough light to make out the slow ripple of a swallow sliding down his throat. "Aye, I do."

His admission had her hoping they might be friends yet, that their joining might be tender and loving. She reached over and touched the bruise on his cheek, wanting to be gentle with him, hoping her kindness would inspire kindness in return. Milread hadn't shaved him, and his beard-roughened skin scored her fingertips.

He flinched beneath her touch. "Before we go any further, answer me one more question, milady."

She drew back, hand shaking. "What is that?"

Looking up at her, his eyes hardened and his mouth slid into a scowl. "Are you so desperate to rut that you must steal unsuspecting men from their sleep?"

The cutting question sliced through the last of Brianna's self-control. "Silence, knave." She hauled back her hand and struck him.

4

CHEEK STINGING, Ewan blinked the water from his eyes. "I ken your redhead's temper hasna softened with the years."

A wise man would hold his tongue rather than invite another slapping or worse, but when had he ever been wise where this woman was concerned? If he'd had a grain of sense, he would have wed one of the pretty, docile lassies of his clan who paraded their charms before him. Instead, he'd remained a bachelor, holding on to the addled hope that Brianna MacLeod might someday step down from her pedestal and be minded of her vow.

The fury blazing from her eyes belied the quivering of her lush lower lip. Even after all these years, he could still remember the sweet, slightly spicy taste of her.

"Speak to me in so vile a fashion again, and I'll have your tongue cut out and fed to the castle curs."

Until now, he'd thought their fair-day meeting might have meant something to her—that *he* might have meant something to her. How very wrong he'd been about that, as well as so many other things. When he'd awakened to find himself chained inside the handsomely appointed private chamber, his clothes whisked away and an old crone sponging him clean, he'd been too confused to make much sense of it all. That Brie had abducted him for the sole purpose of stealing his seed—the cold calculation of such an act was nothing short of heinous.

"You have a verra queer way of wooing, milady. Nay wonder you must set your henchmen to thieving your paramours and binding them to your bed."

She hoisted her chin and arched a brow. "Who said I was wooing you? For the present, you are my property as much as the bed on which you lie or the prized stallion stabled in my paddock."

Crawling out of the shame, he found his voice. "Would you make me your stud and you my broodmare?"

She shrugged. "I want to make a baby with you, Ewan."

Her voice took on that low, sultry tone that brought to mind raw silk and sent his brain buzzing, his heart pounding—and his cock swelling. She stroked her soft hand down the column of his throat, following the path with her nipping mouth and suckling tongue.

Ewan bit his bloodied lip and shifted his head on the pillow, resolving to resist the sensual tease of her full breasts brushing his chest, her braid brushing his lower belly, her thighs chafing his cock and pressing his balls and buttocks deeper into the mattress. "A bastard recognized by neither clan will make for a poor peacemaker."

She frowned down at him. "Our bairn willna be a bastard. As laird, I can legitimize whomever I wish."

"So you dinna mean to marry me, then?" Sarcasm was a poor weapon, but for the time being, it was the only one he had.

Her eyes narrowed. "One husband was more than enough for me."

He hadn't even known she'd wed until her husband turned up dead and she'd blamed his brother for it. Whatever faults Callum had, he was no murderer. Beyond that, Ewan couldn't help feeling that in marrying her cousin, Brie had betrayed him. Their fairday vow might seem like a childish game to her, but to him it had been real, sacred.

Her gaze drifted over him. Ewan had no need to follow that slow, steady perusal. Without looking down, he well knew what she must be seeing. Battered though he was, Brianna's closeness stole his self-control, even as her chains harnessed his strength. Watching her suck at her luscious lower lip brought on a powerful cock stand. And then there were her breasts. Lovely and melon shaped, they taunted him through her shift, reminding him of his bound hands and captive state.

Suddenly, Ewan desperately needed to break the silence. Fixing his gaze on hers, he said, "You're staring." So was he, but that was beside the point.

She shrugged. "And if I am? I went to a great deal of trouble to have you brought here. I want to see what my pains have gained me."

She ran her gaze over him again, slowly, deliberately, and he felt it as keenly as any physical caress. Ewan suspected she was mentally mapping just where and how she would touch him. Being treated thus by a woman, a woman he'd lusted after for years, brought out a tumult of conflicting emotions.

She trailed the tips of two fingers over the seam of

his lips. Despite the bruising, her light touch felt wondrously good. She leaned over him and pressed her mouth to his. He waited for her to speak, but instead she ran the tip of her tongue along that same seam, following the trail her finger had blazed. He heard a groan and was shocked to realize the sound came from him.

She deepened the kiss, drawing his tongue into her mouth. Powerless to stop her, he opened, his tongue twining with hers, his hips lifting off the mattress as far as his chains would allow. She tasted intoxicatingly spicy and sinfully sweet, her lips even softer than he remembered, her clever, stroking tongue leading him to wonder how and if she would kiss him lower.

She pulled back and smiled at him, with her mouth but not her eyes. The latter were as hard and lifeless as the stones their color brought to mind. The first time they'd met, there'd been such light there.

Whatever happened to that braw, bright-eyed lass? he wondered, and then pushed the thought aside. The weight of his chains and the ache in his arms reminded him she was his enemy and not his friend.

She trailed the fingers of one hand over his chest and belly, following the queue of matted hair down to the cloth covering his thighs. Widowhood must explain her shameless lust and bold touch, for she pushed the loincloth away and took him in hand without a trace of hesitation or shame.

Her gaze flew to his. "Good lord, you're hung like a stallion."

Ewan felt his face heat. It was bad enough that he was hard as a brick in her hand without her exclaiming over his size. Fighting to dull his senses and harden his heart—certain other of his parts were hard already—he snared her gaze and said, "You're a witch, Brianna of the MacLeods."

Brianna's face took on a wounded look, but then she dipped her head and turned her attention to toying with the slit at the head of his cock, and he told himself he must have imagined it. She slid the pad of her thumb back and forth. To his shame, he felt himself leaking.

"Like thick rich cream," she murmured, smearing the stickiness over his shaft in deft strokes.

Clenching his jaw to keep from coming, he said, "If you continue on this course, it will be rape." Even as he uttered the word, he couldn't hold back from thrusting into her palm.

"Will it still be rape if I make you desire me?" she asked, again in that soft, slightly husky voice that made his skin prickle and heat.

Truth be told, he already desired her far more than he cared to admit. Still, given his present humiliating circumstances, he wasn't about to give her that satisfaction. "Laird or no, you cannot command desire, my lady."

She shook her head as though giving him up for lost. "I am no unplucked maid, Ewan. I know well enough how to see to a man's pleasure."

It was no idle boast. Each skillful kiss and knowing touch of hers pushed him steadily toward the brink of his self-control. If only he'd had his hands free, he would force her head between his legs and drive his member into the hot hollow of her luscious, lying mouth. Perhaps then he would know peace again, or at least reclaim the ability to think with some semblance of clarity.

Stroking him with nimble fingers, she shook her head as though he were a bairn who'd misbehaved. "There is no point in struggling, my lord. Those chains were forged by my own blacksmith. I assure you the links are quite solid. It does you no good and great harm to struggle so. You but bruise your flesh and aggravate your temper."

"Were I free, I would show you just how aggravated my temper could be—only to your flesh, lady, not mine."

To his chagrin, she smiled. Green eyes glittering, she looked as smug as a cat smacking its lips over a juicy bird it had hobbled and was about to devour. "I have no doubt of it, my lord. Therefore I shall leave you lie just as you are."

Not only was she "no unplucked maid," she was a skilled temptress. Still handling him, she bent her head and laved his nipples, following the soft caress of her tongue with teasing bites that set his blood afire and his heart hammering like a battering ram against his chest.

She released him and glided down his body, the silky rope of her hair brushing over his belly and thighs. Ewan sucked in his breath.

With a hand upon his knee, she looked up at him with wicked eyes. "You can't win, Ewan, and you can't resist. Hold back as long as you will, but in the end I will have you."

He started to answer, but her head disappeared between his open thighs. She slid her lips over him, sheathing him in one velvety wet sweep. In that almost perfect moment, Ewan would have given anything to have his hands free, not to escape but to sink his fingers into the rich silk of her hair.

Heat rolled over his body and pooled in his groin, the exquisite throbbing almost beyond bearing. "Ah, Brie." In the midst of the mounting madness, he forgot he was supposed to hate her.

She drew him deeper still, sucking and laving and pleasuring him, testing the boundaries of his self-control. Though he was under no obligation to act honorably, for whatever reason he couldn't bring himself to seize his release in Brianna MacLeod's sinfully beautiful mouth.

As if sensing he was fast approaching his limit, she pulled back and lifted her shift waist high. A vision of milky-smooth thighs crowned with dark copper curls flitted before him and then she swung a leg over the side of him and bore down. Claiming her seat, she took him inside her in one scalding, slick thrust.

Ewan groaned. Grabbing hold of the headboard, she began to move—back and forth, side to side, and in slow salacious circles that had him gnawing his already swollen lip to keep from crying out. Never before had he known a woman to roll her hips in such a thoroughly beguiling fashion. With each thrust, the exquisite pleasure crested over him like a wave, building toward the pinnacle while whetting his appetite for more.

To distract from it, he reminded himself that Brianna was no longer the innocent girl of his memory, but the MacLeod chief. The enemy's womb would make a poor cradle for his future child. For that reason alone, he ground his teeth and steeled himself to hold back. With luck, she would wear herself out before he weakened.

But Brianna seemed to be a woman who knew not only what she wanted but also how to get it. The single-mindedness of her sensual assault at once aroused his ire and his admiration. She was wearing him down thrust by thrust. Chained or not, surrender was only a matter of time.

He looked up into her face. Perspiration pearled on her forehead and determination darkened her eyes. "Come, damn you." She lowered her head to his and bit his bottom lip, then soothed the sensitized spot with a slow swirl of her tongue.

Pulling back, she looked down upon him, eyes shining in the way he remembered. "Ah, Ewan, it is you who are the tempter among us." Her small sigh filled the space between them. "Surely not even the Archangel Michael could rival your perfection." She reached down and cupped the fruit of his balls in her knowing, kneading hand.

Try as he might, Ewan couldn't hold back any longer. He was neither angel nor saint, but a man, and her canny touch and flexing hips were fast driving him toward madness. The lush body laboring over his, though sheathed in her shift, felt wonderfully feminine, soft yet strong. Moreover, Brianna was no untried maid, but a mature woman who knew her way around a bed. Her long, deep thrusts interspersed with short, quick ripostes were proving too much for his too-long-denied body and weak will to bear.

Like a lightning bolt, the spasm struck fast and

furious, the contractions shattering his will. Surrendering to the storm, Ewan cried out and released his seed inside her.

For some time afterward, seconds or hours he couldn't say, he left his bound body, his senses floating on a sea of peerless, perfect pleasure. A sharp stinging centered in his wrists snapped him back to reality. He opened his eyes to see blood rolling down his forearms. In his climax, he must have yanked on the chains hard enough to send the metal biting into his flesh. Until now, he'd been too lost to the pleasure to notice.

Shame crept in to fill the void where pleasure had resided. He'd just experienced by far the best sexual congress of his life, and it had happened with him a chained captive, a willing slave. The unsparing truth was he'd loved being so used. He turned his face to the wall, but there was no respite to be found there, either. Brianna's silhouette cast a long languorous shadow upon the whitewashed stones.

She used the sleeve of her shift to blot the blood. Ewan snapped his head around.

"Dinna touch me." Chains jangled as he jerked away.

"Ewan?" Her hand settled upon his shoulder, tender now that she'd won her way. "Was it really so terrible that you canna bring yourself to look at me? Did you take no pleasure in it at all?"

Oh, he'd taken pleasure aplenty, only a dark, unholy sort.

Ordinarily, a woman's hurt tone would have softened him at once, but the manacles digging into his wrists and the cramping of his tethered arms reminded him that, like the chains binding him, there was nothing soft about this woman. Brianna of the MacLeods was forged of solid steel.

She stroked a hand along his jaw, as though they were lovers in truth. Had she kept to their blood bargain of ten years before, they might have been bride and groom, and this their wedding night. Thinking of the gentle joining that might have been theirs, Ewan swallowed hard, the rising bitterness burning the back of his throat.

Fixing his gaze upon the canopy, he steeled himself to ruthlessness. "Had you kept to your part of our blood oath, milady, we would have been wed ere now, our clans joined as one. Had you kept to your oath, I would give up my seed to you willingly and not grudgingly. Had you kept to your oath, we might have a nursery full of weans by now. You may get a child by me, but you will get no pleasure from me other than that which you wrest."

Having said his peace, he cut his gaze to her. Tears sparkled in her eyes, spangled her lower lashes. At one time, he would have given an eyetooth for the privilege of being the one to brush away even one precious tear. But even if he had the use of his hands, Brianna MacLeod didn't deserve his compassion.

Staring him down, she firmed her mouth and hardened her eyes. "So be it."

She swung her legs over the side of the bed and rose. Bare feet padded back across the room to where he'd remembered seeing a small writing desk. He closed his eyes and listened to the sounds of her rifling through something, a drawer most likely. Moments later, she

returned to the bed and sat down beside him again.
Ewan opened his eyes—and sucked in his breath.

An eye for an eye...

Light from the sputtering candles above glinted off
the smooth steel blade of a jewel-handled dirk.

EWAN'S EYES WIDENED, but to his credit he didn't flinch.
"Have you found the stomach to kill me after all, milady?"

Brianna affected a shrug, though truth be told her
feelings were hurt. They had just had sexual congress,
an intimate and deeply personal act. She had taken him
into her body, had let him touch the edges of her heart.
Must he persist in believing she meant to murder him
like a black widow killing after coupling?

And yet in the midst of her anger, she couldn't help
admiring him. His eyes, hard as river stones, confirmed
his strength of will more so than the harsh bravado of
his words. Though he was the one of them wearing
chains, he refused to cede so much as an inch of moral
ground. The battle line was as good as drawn. If she
wanted a child from him, she must get it the hard way.
She must wrest his seed from him not once but every
time. So be it.

"Have you no heard that all is fair in love and
war?" she asked.

"Which is this?"

Brianna reached for his hand. "War."

He eyed the knife. "If your intention is to peel me like
an onion and bleed me dry bit by bit, then you'd best
get on with it."

She could have tortured him awhile yet with the

possibility of his demise, but though the treacherous Fraser blood ran thick in his veins, she sensed he was, at heart, a good man. "I confess to having a less mortal wound in mind."

Reaching for him, she turned his hand over and scratched the tip of the blade over the fleshy pad of his thumb, tracing the outline of the thin white scar from ten years before.

Drawing the knife away, she didn't bother with wiping the blade clean. "I've nay wish to do you harm, Ewan. I, too, am minded of our pact made all those many years ago on fair day. Mayhap 'tis time we make another." She held the knife to her left palm and slashed, holding in a wince at the sudden sting.

Hers was the deeper wound, and yet compared to the pain of the past months, it was a trifling thing. She slid her hand into his and laced their fingers, commingling their hearts' blood as they had ten years before. Dutiful daughter though she'd always considered herself to be, were she suddenly to be imbued with Merlin's magic and transported back ten years in time, she would bide in that fair-day barn and let her father's call go unheeded.

Throat thickening with regret, she looked deeply into her prisoner's angry eyes and vowed, "I, Brianna of the MacLeods, do solemnly swear on my father's grave, my husband's grave and most of all on the future of my clan, that once I am with child by you, I will set you free and see you safely back to your people." Putting the knife away, she reclaimed his bloodied hand. "Mind, the first time we so swore, you said we must seal the bargain with a kiss. Will you kiss me now, Ewan?"

Even as she uttered the words, Brianna owned the subtle plea. He was the one of them chained to her bed, captive to her will and wishes. Why then did it feel as though she was the supplicant begging for his favor?

Ewan must have sensed the shift in her. His gaze sharpened. "If you crave more of my kisses, lady, then first free my hands."

Brianna shook her head, not so far gone to her lust as he must think, though the treacherous liquid ache once more trickled between her legs. "That I canna do."

He firmed his lips. "Then you'll get no more kisses from me, lady, other than those you steal."

Once in her life, such a declaration would have put her off, but, God help her, it only fueled her ardor now. She'd ordered Ewan brought to her bed, expecting to sacrifice herself as much as him. He was her sworn enemy, brother to her husband's murderer. To take pleasure in his bound body struck her as obscene, and yet she couldn't help it. She had enjoyed him thoroughly.

"Then I'll have to content myself with the stolen kind…for now." She leaned in and brushed her lips over his.

Like their fair-day encounter, the kiss began slow and sweet. Earlier, she'd seduced him to beget a babe, and though she'd taken sinful pleasure in the act, her higher motive was never far removed from her mind. This kiss, however, was for her alone.

She ran the tip of her tongue across the seam of his mouth, willing him to open, to relinquish his will and submit. This time, however, he held his ground, lips pressed into an unyielding line.

Pulling back, she looked down into his clear determined eyes. "Why should I trust your word or your kiss, milady, when you used both to betray me already?"

Brianna drew back. "I dinna ken your meaning." She had kissed him *after* kidnapping him, not before.

"Do you not? I mind ten years ago how you swore in blood and kisses to wed nay other than me, and yet you broke that oath."

There it was again, that damnable fair-day oath. The blows he'd weathered must have scrambled his wits, for surely he didn't hold her marriage against her? Had she not gone through with wedding Donald, she would have been cast out, disowned. Assuredly, Ewan would have suffered a similar fate at his father and then brother's hands. Without kith or kin to claim them, they would have lived out their lives wandering the countryside as beggars, foraging their daily bread by day and dodging highwaymen and other marauders by night. What manner of legacy would that have been to pass on to their yet-to-be born bairns? As heir, Brianna's first duty was to her clan. Balanced against larger concerns, such selfish human desires as love weighed but slightly.

She was tempted to say as much, but the hour was late, the candles guttering and her heart too tender to risk the onset of any more tears. She glanced away to gather herself.

"We were weans. It was a childish game, nay more." Dear Lord, how she wished that were so.

"Aye, a childish game to be sure." He turned his own face away. "If you've finished with me for the night, I would sleep now."

Brianna hesitated and then stretched out beside him, suddenly shy of brushing bodies now that the act of fornication was through. Should she pull the coverlet over them? she wondered. Marking the sweat still glistening on his chest, she decided against doing so. Certainly, she was more than warm. Swallowing a sigh, she tucked her hands beneath the linen-covered pillow and closed her eyes.

Ewan's voice, hard as river stone, slashed the stillness. "Alone."

Wondering if mayhap she'd misheard, she opened her eyes and lifted her head to look over at him. "Ewan?"

"Surely a stronghold of this size has many more bedchambers than this one." He turned to face her, and the scorn in his eyes assured her she had heard him perfectly. "You have made your bed this night, lady, not I. But as I'm in no position to rise—" he cut a look upward to his chained wrists "—I pray you grant me leave to find what rest I may, *alone.*"

5

AFTER LEAVING HER CHAMBER to Ewan, Brianna fled to her mother's former room overlooking the courtyard. Curled on her side in the center of the big bed, she faced out the open window. Though it was spring, the night breeze was brisk enough to warrant closing the casement, but since crawling beneath the dusty coverlet, Brianna couldn't seem to summon the will to rise. Instead she lay with eyes wide, looking out onto the night. Light from myriad stars and a splendid full moon stabbed through the darkness. The sharpness of that translucent light brought to mind the accusation blazing from Ewan Fraser's clear eyes.

Are you so desperate to rut that you must dispatch your henchmen to steal unsuspecting men from their sleep?

To add insult to injury, he'd called her a witch. Everyone knew witches had long, thinning white hair and warty noses and black, broken teeth. Witches, God help her, looked like Milread, who was reputed to be one. Brianna had long ago made peace with the fact she was no beauty, but being likened to one of Satan's hand-maids struck a mighty blow to her already wounded female pride.

She hugged the velvet-covered pillow tight against her middle, her only defense against the emptiness. Fairday plighting of troths aside, she wished she'd found another way to end the feud so that she might have left Ewan Fraser be. But the damage was done. The kidnapping had been carried out and so had the bedding. Though it wasn't possible to deflower a man, and she felt certain Ewan was no virgin, she'd as good as committed rape. She couldn't recall if rape counted as a venial sin or a mortal one, but either way, her behavior was bad, if not exactly heinous. She only hoped her sin would bear fruit without requiring much repeating. After the cruelties they'd traded this night, bedding Ewan a second time promised to be even harder than the first.

Lying alone with such weighty thoughts made for a long and restless night. Brianna's eyelids grew heavy just as the first thin streaks of dawn lightened the sky. Giving in to exhaustion, she slept. A black-haired boy with moonstone-colored eyes and Ewan's old flute danced through her dreams, only he wasn't Ewan, but the son they'd made together. She awoke to wailing—hers—and the sensation of warm treacle flowing between her legs.

Her courses had begun.

Ewan Fraser would be her "guest" for another month at least.

Ewan likewise lay awake to see dawn lights streaking through the window, the scent of sex, spring flowers and Brianna filling his nostrils and fogging his thoughts. He hadn't really expected her to honor his request to leave,

but he'd been glad for the chance to collect his badly shattered composure. Before going, she'd covered him with a quilt and murmured promises of longer chains, warm clothing and a proper meal to come on the morrow. Given the harsh words they'd exchanged, he wasn't certain how to trust such tenderness.

And yet aside from the restraints, his current accommodations were a far cry from the freezing dungeon cell he'd expected. To distract from the ache in his arms, he sent his gaze on a slow perusal of the room. The chamber wasn't overlarge, but it was handsomely furnished, as befitting a laird's private abode. The bed upon which he lay was high and broad enough to accommodate an entire peasant family, the mattress beneath his battered back pleasantly firm, yet soft, as if stuffed with goose feathers rather than straw or horsehair or bracken. Next to the bed sat a long red chest of the type typically used to store folded clothing. An ornate metal strongbox, conspicuously padlocked, occupied the far end. There was also a round table with a chessboard and pieces atop, and a writing desk, of the small, delicately carved kind favored by noblewomen. Lifting his head, Ewan saw that the quill had been left out, its black ink bleeding into a stack of clean sheets as though the owner had suffered some interruption while in the act of composing. His lady laird must ken her letters.

Brie could read and write! Fury bubbled up within him and then burst like a plague boil, putrid and reeking. He gritted his teeth to keep from crying out, and wished with all his heart he might find his hands free in order to break the innocent little desk into a thousand splintered pieces.

Over the years, he'd sent her numerous notes written in his less than tidy hand and dispatched by way of traveling tradesmen and troubadours headed for the MacLeod great hall. One letter, saints preserve him, had included a pitiful little poem likening her hair to flames and her skin to sweet cream. None had met with any answer. At first he'd tried telling himself that the messages must have been intercepted or lost, then later that she must not have the art of reading them. Seeing the writing desk confirmed what he'd always known in his heart.

Brianna MacLeod didn't give a tinker's damn about him.

And yet there was no denying that her lush full lips had felt mightily good cinched about his cock, her pretty pink tongue and nibbling white teeth adept at arousing sensations he'd never before experienced in such a completely consuming way. Still, he hadn't realized how very lost he was until the moment she'd mounted him, her slender white thighs squeezing as though he were a stallion she'd set out to break. And break him she had. Scalding and slippery as marsh grass, her sex had grasped him like a tight-fisted glove, the movements of her tight arse and softly curved hips daring him to deny his pleasure or hers. When he'd finally surrendered, his climax was more potent than any previous release.

The erotic thoughts had him thickening, and he gritted his teeth again, this time turning the fury upon himself. He was a weakling where Brianna was concerned, a traitor to his honor and his clan, a slave to desire—his as well as hers. Should she come back to claim him a second time, there would be no question of rape. He would be more than willing to accommodate her.

And yet even admitting he'd just had the most satisfying sexual encounter of his life, he couldn't help feeling he'd lost something. Until now, Brianna had existed as his golden girl, an unblemished memory. Their fair-day kiss, clumsy though he'd been, ranked as one of the most perfect moments of his life.

We were weans. It was a childish game, nay more.

Those words had left a far greater sting than the slashing of her dirk against his palm or the manacles shaving the skin from his wrists.

She hadn't abducted him because she wanted him for her husband or even her lover. She wanted only one thing from him—a baby. Well, he wanted something from her, too, and it was no longer her hand in marriage or her heart. It was his freedom.

The kirtle circling her slender waist held many keys, and one of them surely must fit the lock to his fetters. She'd come to bed in only her shift and then dressed again before leaving him for the night. The keys would have gone with her, of course. Still, it was maddening to consider that the means to his liberty might have been so very near and yet still out of reach.

Jaw clenched, he vowed to do whatever it took to get that key.

AFTER THE DISTURBING DREAM, Brianna slipped into a short but mindless sleep. She awoke to the cock crowing in the courtyard below, and it took her a moment to remember she wasn't in her chamber, but in her mother's. Groggy and blinking, she got up and made her toilet as best she could, finger combing her hair and taming it into a makeshift plait, rinsing her mouth and dressing in the previous day's clothes. Glimpsing her bare throat in the dressing mirror, she realized that before leaving the night before she'd forgotten to replace the seal ring about her neck. She'd left it in her desk drawer along with the letter to Callum Fraser she'd decided against sending.

Milread's warning returned in a rush. *The laird's seal isna safe anywhere but on your person.*

For a handful of seconds, panic flared, but Brianna tamped it down. The ring should be safe enough until she retrieved it later. True, she'd left the desk unlocked, but the sentry stood guard outside the chamber door, and Ewan was, after all, chained. Given all he'd endured in the past twenty-four hours, she suspected he slept still.

Ewan. Her heart clenched. She'd anticipated he'd be furious over his abduction and rough handling. What she hadn't foreseen was his bitterness over her broken vow. That he loathed her was abundantly clear. Whether he was captive or free, bedding her was the very last thing he desired.

She threw herself into her duties for the day, hoping to clear her mind, or at least distract herself from her troubles for a little while at least. Laird though she was, she had served as her father's chatelaine since her mother's death. Whatever other faults she possessed, she'd never been a shirker. By noon, she'd taken inventory of the stillroom and dairy and poked her head inside the bake house.

Whenever Ewan entered her thoughts, she forced herself to focus on happier, or at least less complicated, matters. She might be a dismal failure as a woman, but as a leader she was slowly but surely stepping in to fill her father's shoes. Up until Ewan's bursting in, her first court day as laird had gone exceedingly well. In Alys's case especially, justice had been served.

Now that Alasdair was returned to his rightful mother, Brianna considered that the baby snatching might have been a blessing in disguise. Had Alys not come before Brianna's court to reclaim her kidnapped child, she would still be plying her trade on the streets. The latter would be a tragedy indeed. Young, pretty and seemingly wise beyond her years, the girl could do a great deal more with her life. Who knew, but mayhap some bold but kindhearted warrior would take a fancy to her and make her his lady wife? It could happen.

Spinning a fairy-tale future for Alys distracted Brianna from her problems, but only for a short while. She couldn't banish the previous painful night from her mind indefinitely. Images flooded her, the recent erotic memory laden with a bevy of emotions both angry and sad.

The onset of her courses would prevent her and Ewan lying together for several more days. The sooner she had his baby in her belly, the sooner she could return him to his clan and end the feud. Once they began sleeping together regularly, she doubted the pregnancy would take long to bring about. She'd already shown she could conceive, and unlike Donald, Ewan was a passionate man. By the next full moon, she fully expected to find herself with child. For all their sakes, she heartily hoped that proved to be the case. Ewan's appearance in her great hall guaranteed that word of his capture would reach his brother's ear before long. For all she knew, it had already. Though she'd never met the cur, she couldn't believe Callum Fraser would allow his twin to be kept captive indefinitely.

Her wandering footfalls carried her toward the kitchen, where she spotted Milread within the low-walled garden. Entering through the lichen-covered gate, she saw the serving woman was at work on the plot set aside for her special healing herbs, hoeing dirt about a row of some shiny, leafy plants. Nearly sightless, Milread had a canny knack for coaxing forth lush growth. Brianna had never seen the like.

The gate closed with a squeak, but apparently Milread was too absorbed in her work to note it. Either that or the poor old dear must be growing deaf. Rather than startle her, Brianna made her way toward the bench, her slippers nearly soundless on the stone pavers, and took a seat. In no particular hurry, she propped her elbows on her knees, held her chin in her hands and settled in to wait.

"Why so sad, sweeting?"

Startled, Brianna jolted upright. "Who says I'm sad?"

The old woman left off raking and leaned down stiffly to inspect her handiwork. Pinching off a leaf, she held it to her nose and sniffed. "I'll never forget the sight of your wee face the day you came back from that fair day with your da and showed me that wee scabbed-over knife cut upon your thumb. When I asked whatever had happened, you whispered you'd met the lad who was your true love and that you'd sworn in blood to wed. I could still see somewhat back then, and the shine in your eyes fair near to blinded me." Milread popped the leaf—basil, or so it looked to Brianna—into her mouth and munched.

Brianna swallowed hard, emotion thickening her throat. Like a feeble fire that needed near constant watching, she'd kept that fair-day memory alive for a decade now, had breathed life into it whenever it had shown signs of fading. After last night, it was lost to her—lost as so many precious things were.

She dropped her gaze to the hands lying clenched in her lap. "That was a long time ago. It has nothing to do with bringing Ewan to my bed."

Milread rose on creaking knees and turned about. Brianna started to go and help her, but the wise woman hissed and waved her away.

Using the hoe as a staff, she leaned forward and shook her head. "Mayhap it does and mayhap it doesna, but surely a strapping warrior such as Ewan Fraser wouldna let a few fight marks keep him from doing his duty by a woman he once fancied sufficient to wed?"

Brianna managed a glum nod. "He did his duty, albeit grudgingly. Mind, I was a lassie when we met. Now I am a woman grown tall and stout as a tree."

Milread scowled. "Och, you're pretty as a picture and fresh as a flower. As for stout, it's curved you are in all the proper places." Her murky gaze settled on Brianna's breasts.

No longer able to sit still, Brianna shot to her feet. Hands fisted at her sides, she began to pace.

"He doesna desire me. He blames me for breaking our vow. He hates me for having him kidnapped. He did everything he could to hold himself back from giving me a baby. After he…finished, he wouldna look at me for the longest while, and when he did, it was only loathing I saw in his eyes."

Head cocked, Milread chewed thoughtfully. A knot appeared and then disappeared in her throat as she swallowed the vestiges of the leaf. "I vow it wasna loathing you saw, wean, but shame at his own weakness. A man's pride is a verra fragile thing."

It was Brianna's turn to scoff. If that were so, then Ewan Fraser wasn't the only one who'd awoken with hurt pride this morning. Rounding on her nurse, she admitted, "He said that if I continued on my course, it would be rape." The bitterness lacing Brianna's voice took her aback. Until now, she hadn't realized how very much those words had hurt.

Scowling, the wise woman threw down the hoe. "Och, that will never do. A child conceived of rape will be born with a black stain upon its soul."

Brianna felt on the verge of throwing up her hands. If what Milread said was true, then the commencement of her courses was a blessing. Her future child was to be her clan's savior, not its destroyer. And yet there was no reason to believe Ewan would be any fonder of her when her flow ended than he had been on the previous night. After spending successive days in chains—even lengthier, more comfortable chains—he might like her a good deal less.

"What can I do?"

The crone's weathered face softened. Mischief glinted in her murky gaze. Dropping her voice to a high whisper, she answered, "Woo him, my lady. Win him to you with gentle touches and not-so-gentle bites and scratches. Lick and suckle and tease him until he is so mad for you he begs you to stop and never stop all in the same breath. Pleasure him thus, and you shall be pleasured in turn."

Face warming as though she'd downed a cup of strong wine in a single swallow, Brianna looked away lest Milread suspect her shameful secret. The night before, she hadn't climaxed. Intent on pleasuring Ewan so that he would spend himself inside her, she'd forgone her own fulfillment. In striving to please him, she had driven herself half-mad with wanting.

But beyond all those cares and concerns and excuses lay her deepest, darkest, saddest secret of all. She'd never once known a climax. Neither her own hand nor Donald's halfhearted fumbling had brought about the longed-for release. Faith, she wasn't certain she even understood what such release meant, though it must be a wondrous thing. For the first time it struck her that mayhap she had the right to feel more than a little wronged, a lot cheated. What the lowliest peasant woman claimed as her due Brianna had never so much as sampled.

She sank back down onto the bench seat. Imagining Milread must have used her powers to peer into her invisible "third eye" and there read her shameful secret, she looked away. "What possible difference can my pleasure or Ewan's make to an unborn babe?"

Milread brought her wrinkled face down close, her basil-scented breath striking Brianna's nose. "If he gives up his seed willingly, not grudgingly, once planted in your womb, it will bear fair fruit, not foul."

Brianna's heart dipped. Only now did she admit she'd sought out Milread hoping for a love potion or at least an aphrodisiac to heighten Ewan's physical desire. This once, though, the crone didn't seem inclined to offer it, and Brianna was too proud to ask. She scoured her brain for some simple home remedy she might know already. Ingesting oysters raw from the shell was said to increase a man's potency and desire. Should she feed her captive consort oysters? No, she decided. The uncooked shellfish, though prized as a delicacy, carried too great a risk. She'd heard of men rising from the table with a virulent bellyache, plagued by the runs until, unable to take in food or drink, they wasted away. Even if he was her sworn enemy, she wasn't willing to risk Ewan's life. Besides, it wasn't his potency that needed remedying—she'd been amazed at how long he'd lasted—but rather his desire.

Milread's rasp broke into her thoughts, answering her unspoken question yet again. "The key to winning the Fraser lies not in potions and spells but in the womanly power that lies within you already."

Brianna rubbed her brow where a dull headache drummed. "You speak in riddles."

Milread's violent shake of her head sent wispy white hair flying. "Whisht, child, it is your pride that has stopped up your ears. To seduce his body and soften his heart, you must first play with him."

Brianna glanced up abruptly. "Play with him?"

"Aye, play with him and give him leave to play with you in turn." Leaning heavily on the handle of her hoe, the wise woman speared Brianna with her steady, unblinking gaze. "Coupling need not be a somber affair. Play as though you were weans still. That was how it was between you two when you first met, was it not? Playful and wild and...*free?*" With a wink, Milread turned about, picked up the hoe and resumed her raking, leaving Brianna to her thoughts.

Was the wise woman's mention of freedom a veiled reference to her having Ewan chained? she wondered. If so, she conceded Milread might have a point. Iron fetters were hardly the way to forge goodwill. Recalling his raw, bloodied wrists, she felt guilt wash over her. And yet Ewan was a powerfully built man, as well as rightfully furious with her. If she freed his hands, what was to keep him from locking them about her throat? She doubted he would murder a woman, even her, in cold blood, but once he overpowered her, what was to keep him from taking her as his hostage?

She'd opened her mouth to press for more answers when Alys entered the garden, Alasdair in her arms. Coming from the direction of the dairy, she had a crisp white apron covering the front of her yellow gown.

"Hullo, Alys. How fare you this day?"

Brianna ran her gaze over the girl. When she wasn't looking like a wild thing poised to flee, Alys really was very pretty, petite and fair-haired, with a high forehead, violet-blue eyes and a perfect rosebud mouth. Reminded of her own too-wide, too-full lips, Brianna felt a pang of envy. Chained or not, Ewan likely wouldn't think twice about accepting Alys's advances. That the girl was also schooled in the erotic arts had Brianna feeling even poorer by comparison. Ewan must have found her desperate, clumsy efforts to please pathetic indeed.

Cheeks flushed, Alys halted in midstep. "I am well, milady. But forgive me, I didna mean to disturb you. Alasdair is not yet weaned, and I thought to sit in the sunshine and feed him." She began backing away to the gate.

"You are welcome to remain."

Twisting her head about, Milread interjected, "Aye, stay you, mistress. We have need of your skills."

Alys stopped. "My skills?"

Milread threw down the hoe and ambled over to them. "Aye, in the art of love."

Wave upon wave of horrified heat rolled over Brianna. She reached out and plucked the old woman's sleeve as she had when she was a child, only instead of a confection from the kitchen or a story before bed, it was Milread's discretion she wanted. That she'd had to face the guard, Seamus, a second time the previous night brought humiliation aplenty. She didn't need the servants snickering behind her back.

Shrugging free, Milread lowered herself onto the stone slab. She gestured Alys to the vacant space on Brianna's other side. "Sit you, mistress, for we have need of your counsel."

Alys hesitated and then joined them on the bench. As soon as she did, Alasdair began to kick and fuss. She sat him down upon the ground to play. Immediately he began amusing himself with pulling up fistfuls of grass and wildflowers.

Once everyone was settled, Milread came directly to the point. "We have a problem. In order to end the feud with the Frasers, my lady must get a bairn from Ewan Fraser whilst she holds him here. So far, he will not willingly give up his seed."

Alys cast a nervous look at Brianna and then dropped her gaze to her clasped hands, lying white-knuckled in her lap. "Aye, I had heard the talk."

It was not yet noon, and already the gossip had made the rounds. Though Ewan was her prisoner, kept nearly naked and in chains, she felt as though she were the one who'd been stripped bare. Unable to meet either woman's eye, Brianna dropped her gaze to her slipper-shod feet, big and long-boned as the rest of her. Were she pert-featured and petite like Alys, she felt certain bedding Ewan would have gone a great deal better than it had. But she couldn't help her face or her size any more than she could help her red hair.

To make Ewan desire her, she was going to need a little help from her friends.

A sideways glance to Alys showed the color in the girl's cheeks to be deepening, but to her credit she didn't look away. Leaning forward, she divided her gaze between Milread and Brianna. "I dinna ken what it is you wish to know, but whatever knowledge I've gained I'll gladly share."

Tossing Brianna a look, Milread answered for them both. "Well, to begin, mayhap you could advise milady on what a man finds most pleasing to the eye."

Alys bit her lip as though considering whether or not to answer. Turning to Brianna, she skimmed her blue eyes over her hair, her face. "Well, you have verra lovely hair, milady, but you might think about wearing it in a different style."

Self-conscious, Brianna fingered her haphazard plait. "This way keeps it out of my face as I go about my day."

Milread jabbed her in the ribs. "It isna your days we need concern ourselves with but your nights."

Alys cleared her throat. "No doubt it's very practical for the daytime, as Mistress Milread says. But in my...experience, men fancy hair they can slide their fingers through."

Putting her pride aside, Brianna asked, "What do you suggest?"

Alys studied her. Like a wee general taking command, she reached for her braid and unwound the leather thong holding the end. Finger combing the waves, she appeared to be taking stock of the possibilities.

At length, she said, "Perhaps we might affect some light braiding at the crown, like a coronet, but leave the rest long and flowing."

It was clear that the "we" would be Alys. Milread, for all her canniness with potions and divination and gardening, had no aptitude for dressing hair, not even her own. Brianna feared she was likewise a lost cause. By the time she'd become interested in things such as hair and cosmetics and clothing, her mother lay in the kirkyard. Without sisters or female cousins to school her, she'd reached womanhood with little knowledge of the feminine arts. Until now she'd dismissed such womanly wiles as a waste of time. Why should she put herself to the trouble of looking pretty when her husband never looked at her at all? Now it occurred to her to wonder if perhaps she wasn't missing out on an important part of being a woman.

Milread's words from the day before returned to her with new meaning. *You already ken what it means to be a laird. 'Tis time to go forth and be a woman.*

Was it possible to incite a man's passion as well as hold his respect? In the past, she'd assumed she must settle for one or the other. She'd wed Donald because he had been her father's choice. Until now she'd tried telling herself that sexual congress was a means to an end, no more, but having been with Ewan, she was no longer so sure. Begetting a child was still the result she sought, but she was beginning to suspect that pleasure, a great deal of it, could be derived from the act. Inexperienced as she was, she sensed the night before was but a bite-size morsel of what might be a bountiful feast if only she could find a way to make Ewan hunger for her as she did for him. For that to happen, she needed him to see her not as his captor nor the girl of his memory, but as a woman.

Alys's soft voice broke into her thoughts. "And you also might wish to consider a slimmer-fitting gown."

Startled, Brianna demanded, "What is the matter with my gown?"

The green garment was perfectly serviceable, its free-flowing folds allowing her to go about her household chores unencumbered. Beyond that, she fancied it hid her…largesse in certain areas.

Milread, not Alys, answered, "It puts me in mind of a granary sack you nicked from yonder mill house."

And this from a near-blind woman!

Ever the diplomat, Alys intervened. "The color is lovely with your eyes, milady, but the gown is a wee bit…bulky. You have a handsome figure with a fine full bosom and a supple waist, but garbed as you are we canna see it…nor can Lord Ewan."

Brianna thought for a moment. She'd sought advice and she had received it. "I ken you fancy working in the dairy, but how would you feel about serving as my personal maid? As I've never had a woman to wait upon me, I daresay I won't be too demanding. You shall have plenty of time to care for Alasdair and to help out in the dairy if you wish."

"Truly, milady?" Alys clapped her small hands, clearly delighted.

Brianna nodded. "Aye, it seems I could use the help. You and Alasdair can move into the dressing chamber adjoining mine. Not the laird's solar, but my mother's old chamber," she added quickly. "It is in the south tower overlooking the courtyard. Milread can show you the way."

Predictably, the admission that she and Ewan were sleeping in separate chambers sent sympathetic glances her way. But there was no point in dissembling. It was clear to all that the bedding had been a disaster.

An awkward silence descended. For a moment the only sounds to fill it were Alasdair's baby cooing, the cawing of a rook roosting on the wall and the bleating of the lamb in the nearby pen.

Milread cleared her throat. Pinning her sightless gaze on Brianna's profile, she addressed Alys. "Now that we have settled on how to please Lord Ewan's eyes, let us address the weightier subject of how to soften his heart and coax his desire into full bloom."

The three women put their heads together. Brianna found some of Alys's suggestions shocking indeed. Widow though she was, she had not suspected there were quite so many variations on giving and receiving pleasure. Still, she had to admit that committing those carnal acts with not just any man, but with Ewan Fraser, was an arousing prospect. Though she sat on a garden bench between two women, a baby playing at their feet, she felt her breasts straining against her lacings and her sex strumming like an instrument yearning to be played.

Glancing down at the bairn, Brianna was mightily glad wee Alasdair was as yet too young to speak. Addressing such worldly matters within earshot of an innocent child who might later parrot them back brought heat searing her cheeks. Still, if she succeeded in seducing Ewan, body and heart, she soon might find herself a happy mother-to-be. She might not be able to transform herself into a siren overnight, but putting into play Alys's and Milread's "advice," coupled with softening her appearance, could only help matters. Regardless of the result, it fell to her to try.

She'd come too far to turn back now.

6

MINDED OF HER PROMISE to feed Ewan a proper meal, Brianna left Milread and Alys in the garden and headed down the path to the stone kitchen. Preparations for the midday repast halted as soon as she crossed the threshold. Understandably the pie-faced cook was flustered to have the laird simply stroll inside her culinary domain, but Brianna quickly set her at ease, reminding her they were old acquaintances. She might no longer be the plump lassie who pilfered pies and cakes cooling in the window well, but she still appreciated a light, flaky crust as much as she ever had. The older woman broke into a yellow-toothed smile and snapped her fingers to the kitchen maids. Within a short time, Brianna had a basket packed with delicacies. Rather than delegate the task to a servant, she resolved to feed Ewan herself.

Sometime later, she entered the laird's bedchamber, the door opened by a different guardsman stationed outside. Thankful to be spared the shame of having to face Seamus's smirking look, she sailed inside.

She found Ewan much as she'd left him, lying with his head propped on pillows. With daylight streaming into the chamber, she took the opportunity to study him.

The cuts and lacerations were still pronounced, but she fancied the swelling had gone down considerably over-night. Though she'd left him mere hours before, it felt as if a lifetime had passed. The slight soreness settling between her thighs reminded her it had been some time since she'd been with a man. Compared to the…*bounty* of Ewan Fraser, Donald had been modestly endowed. Ewan was not only long, but delectably thick, his member shaped to fit a woman's hand and mouth and nether parts. When she'd stroked him, her own sex had thrummed and moistened in response, and her skin had felt flushed as if with fever.

Determined to banish the previous night from her mind, she summoned a sunny smile and asked, "How do you fare this day?"

Ewan answered with a scowl. "How would you fare, milady, if you were beaten, half-starved, violated and then watched over by a booby-eyed beastie?"

Glancing to the "booby-eyed beastie" making his bed on the pillow beside Ewan's dark head, Brianna chuckled. "I see you've met Lord Muffin."

He turned to cast the cat a skeptical glance. "'Tis bad enough you've chained me like a dog, but must you set your devil cat to guard me, as well?"

Donald had disliked Muffin, indeed all cats. To be fair, it wasn't so much dislike as a keen physical reaction. Coming into contact with the fur had resulted in the swollen eyes and stuffy nose associated with a head cold. Once he and Brianna had wed, Muffin had been banished from her bedchamber. Upon Donald's death, one of the first things she had done was to bring back her feline friend. A cat was no substitute for a lover, but having that warm, furry body lying next to her at night had taken the edge off the loneliness.

Approaching, Brianna hid a smile and reached out to stroke her pet. "I thought you liked cats. At the very least, they don't make you sneeze." She stopped, embarrassed that she might have betrayed just how thoroughly she'd committed their fair-day meeting to memory. To distract him, she quickly added, "Besides, Muffin here is coming on thirteen, so he's no threat."

Ewan snorted. "So say you. I'm no all that keen to have my eyes scratched out of my skull."

Continuing to stroke the cat's patchy fur, she answered, "He's only ever scratched when someone has tried picking him up. Otherwise he's the gentlest of animals. And he seems to have taken a fancy to you."

"I ken it's your pillow he fancies. It holds your scent."

"My scent?" Brianna had no patience for fripperies such as costly perfumes from France. Even if she had, with many of her clansmen living so meanly in the present troubled times, how could she justify the indulgence?

"Aye, you smell of lavender and cherry blossoms and something else—something that's just…you."

She hesitated and then took a seat on the side of the bed, laying the basket in her lap. "Milread makes a special goat's milk soap I use to bathe."

Upon leaving the kitchen, she'd stopped by her mother's chamber to wash and to tidy her hair.

"It's…nice."

Flustered, she looked away. "Thank you."

Biting her bottom lip, she reminded herself she was

a laird as well as a widow. It was unseemly for a seasoned woman such as herself to behave so very foolishly, but Ewan Fraser had a canny knack for making her forget herself.

He stared at the basket. "Don't tell me you've brought more healing unguents? Faith, milady, you are the very soul of compassion." Sarcasm underscored his tone.

Determined to ignore it, she lifted the wicker lid. "I thought you might be eager to break your fast, and last night I did promise you a proper meal." Her mention of the embarrassing episode had her inwardly wincing.

"It seems The MacLeod is a woman of her word…in *some* matters." He flicked his gaze to his chained wrists.

Brianna steeled herself. "Some favors must be earned, milord."

"I would have thought I had done so last night."

Resolved not to let him bait her, and thereby lose all her good intentions so early in the day, Brianna turned her attention to the cloth-wrapped bundles in her basket. Aware of his eyes raking over her, she felt her heart skipping beats and her fingers growing clumsy.

"Sustenance but not freedom, is that your game, milady? With one hand you give and with the other you take away." His sharp tone cut her as though he was a diamond and she made of glass.

She forced a shrug. "It serves my purpose to see that you do not starve."

"Feed me, then. Or is setting food before a half-starved man who canna reach to take it yet another of your torturer's tricks?"

She let out a sigh, feeling her good mood slipping. "Why must you always think the worst of me?"

Glaring eyes met hers. "Why indeed." He deliberately moved his arms, setting the chains rattling.

Rather than argue with him, she broke off a bite of oatcake and held it to his lips. He hesitated and then opened his mouth for her.

"This is good." Swallowing, he lifted his head, looking for more.

Hoping he hadn't guessed the direction of her thoughts, she broke off a morsel of smoked salmon and fed it to him. "You're insatiable."

Chewing, he shrugged. "Unchain me, and then there's nay reason for you to serve me."

"I don't mind serving you." She said so as a courtesy, and yet she realized it was the truth. Despite the awkwardness between them, she was rather enjoying herself.

She tore off another morsel and fed it to him. His lips slid over her finger much as hers had slid over his shaft the night before. Brianna shivered, a warm chill striking her spine and lower belly.

She dropped her voice to ask, "What mischief are you about, Ewan Fraser?"

"Why, breakfast, milady. What else?" The wicked gleam in his eye belied the innocence of the question. "It's rare tasty, too." He teased his tongue over her digit's sensitive tip, and she felt a splash of warmth between her thighs.

Pressing her legs firmly together, she shook her head. "I ken you're no longer fashing yourself that I've set out to poison you." She arched a brow.

"You may yet, lady, but after last night, I ken you've use for me still." He had the audacity to wink.

Now that his vigor was returning, Brianna could see he was something of a rogue when it came to women. Despite his resistance the night before, he was a very sensual man. She, on the other hand, was a novice in love play, for all that she was a widow and older than him. The night before, she'd drawn mainly on instinct and her own deep-seated desire. As illuminating as the morning's talk with Alys had been, there was no substitute for experience.

"I can please you, my lady." Clear eyes with a hint of the devil in them looked up into hers. "Unchain my hands and let me show you."

Ah, so that was his game. Make her crave his touch and then cajole her into releasing him. And yet meeting his moonstone gaze, how she wanted to believe him. Heaven alone knew how she wished to believe he might desire her as much as she wanted him, to feel the warmth and roughness of his hands caressing her body, the weight of him pressing her into the rope mattress in the most delicious of ways, to savor the slapping of his damp, hard-muscled flesh against hers as he drove himself into her again and again. But the part of her brain still capable of reason couldn't overlook the obvious ruse. If she freed him, he could overpower her in a heartbeat. What was to stop him from wresting the dirk from her garter and slitting her throat or, worse yet, taking her hostage? As much as she was a woman with a woman's wants, she was first and foremost a laird to her people.

"You're a knave, Ewan Fraser, as well as my sworn enemy. Give me but one reason why I should trust you."

He didn't as much as blink. "After last night, we're as good as handfast wed. That makes me your lord and master for the coming year and a day."

"Lord and master, indeed!" In the midst of her frustration, she tossed back her head and laughed. She couldn't help it. Such arrogance in one so young and in such straits was too absurd to go ignored. "Before pride tempts you to call yourself so again, you might well mark which of us is wearing prison irons."

"Sex isna the same as lovemaking." If possible, the scowl he shot her only rendered him that much more beautiful. "Unbind me, Brianna. Unbind me and I vow I'll show you the sun and moon and stars."

She hesitated, the woman within her warring with the laird. The novelty of fornicating with a fettered man was rapidly wearing thin. She wanted—needed—to feel his hands on her body.

Ewan must have sensed her wavering. "Last night when you stroked me between my legs with your deft, slender hand, I could scarce hold back from coming. I want to do that to you, Brie. I want to fondle you and finger you until you canna stand it another second. I want you to come in my hand and then I want to take you with my mouth and later my cock and make you come again and again. But I canna do so trussed like livestock. Let me show you how good it can be. How good *we* can be. Give me leave, milady. Give me leave."

Feeling as though she'd been plunged into a too-warm bath, Brianna held up a perspiring palm. "Ewan, cease."

Apparently resolved to be relentless, he hardened his eyes and shook his head. "I want to play bitch-and-hound with you, turn you over upon your hands and knees and rut within you until you scream from the pleasure of it."

Scalding heat washed over her. He might not have the use of his hands, but his glib tongue was every whit as cunning as that of the serpent that had tempted Eve. Alarmed by the liquid warmth pooling between her thighs, Brianna covered her ears, seeking to escape the wicked thrill.

"Stop it. I won't listen to another word. You…you should be ashamed of yourself."

"*I* should be ashamed? That's rich when 'twas you who had me kidnapped and brought here for the sole purpose of servicing you."

Brianna felt her face flame. "I brought you here so I might conceive a child who would carry the blood of both our clans, to restore peace to our peoples. Peace your brother destroyed."

"For the final time, my brother didna murder your husband! Unchain me and I'll find a way to prove it." The force of the shouted demand lifted his upper body from the bed.

"Then how do you explain the scrap of clothing found in my…in Donald's hand?"

"It must have been stolen." Ewan subsided back on the mattress.

Brianna glared at him. "How…convenient."

He hoisted a dark brow and pinned her with his unnerving gaze. "Tell me, milady, is bloodlust the only thing you crave? Do you want nothing for yourself?"

Wondering what manner of game he played, Brianna answered with care. "I want a baby to end the feud, but then you know this already."

He lanced her with an openly skeptical look. "You are laird, true, but you are also a woman. Can you honestly say you don't crave pleasure from the act? Surely you must want more than a callous coupling?"

Ashamed at how very much more she did want from him, she looked away. "My pleasure is beside the point."

"Is it? And yet I fancy you would love the feeling of my fingers toying with those lovely, long nipples I felt against my chest through your smock last night. Imagine what it would be like, Brianna, to look down and see my head buried between your sweet thighs, to feel my tongue coaxing the cream from your body."

Frustrated tears burned the backs of her eyes. Though she hadn't climaxed last night, still she'd found pleasure such as she'd never before known existed. How cruel to taunt her with the outward signs of her satisfaction, her complete abandonment to the pleasure, to him.

She shook her head, vowing that whatever pleasure she might find in the future she would keep to herself. "Give me a child, Ewan. A child is all I ask of you. Once you have planted your seed in me, you have my word I will release you to your murderous brother. We need never meet again."

Before she might be tempted to recant, she rose and left the room.

Only after she stepped out into the hallway did she realize that once again she'd left her ring behind.

CALLUM FRASER SNAPPED upright in his bed, drawing a cry of complaint from the buxom doxy plastered to his side. For the second night in a row, he woke up from a sound sleep feeling as if his whole body had been trampled. The sheet was a tangled mess at his feet, his bared body bathed in sweat and his heartbeat furious and fast as though he'd just run a race. His shoulders and arms suffered particular pain. He felt as strained and stiff as though an unseen hand had stretched him upon the rack. At the base of his skull, a dull headache throbbed. He felt his forehead for fever, but found it perfectly cool. He wasn't ill.

When Ewan hadn't returned home the day before as planned, neither Callum nor anyone else had been unduly alarmed. Since they were boys, his twin had had a habit of going off on his own for days at a stretch. Ewan didn't mark time as other men did. An overnight jaunt to camp upon the shores of the loch might stretch on to a sennight. In that respect, his brother was a wee bit fey. Ewan was content to sit in silence for hours on end observing the various species of birds and other wild creatures that made their home on the loch. For Callum the sole purpose of such an excursion was to bring home meat for the table or a trophy for the wall. On one occasion years before, Ewan had returned jubilant over having spotted a rare white-tailed sea eagle flying over the loch. Given the season, the animal must have a nest nearby. Equally excited, Callum had grabbed his bow and arrow and rushed out to slay the bird. When he brought it back home, his brother had refused to speak to him for a full month.

They were so different that betimes it was difficult to

imagine they'd shared their mother's womb. Still, they were brothers, twins. Their tastes and temperaments were as opposite as night was to day, and yet there was a canny connection between them. Callum would never forget the time when they were very young, maybe five or six, and he had sneaked into the kitchen to steal a slice of the roasting pig. The knife had been unwieldy for so small a hand, and he'd sawed off a part of his middle finger instead. Ewan had been on the other side of the courtyard playing when he'd suddenly experienced a stabbing sensation in the very same digit.

Try as he might to tell himself there was no reason for alarm now, Callum knew in his gut that the very opposite was true. Ewan was in trouble. He also sensed his twin was very much alive. The latter brought him some comfort, though his sense of urgency did not abate. Fortunately, he was well acquainted with the remote inlet that was his brother's special spot.

Resolved, he swung his long legs over the side of the bed and reached for his discarded plaid. He wrapped the material about himself and rose. His manservant slept on a cot in the clothing cupboard next door. Rousing the lackey, he sent him for water so that he might shave and wash the fear-scented sweat from his skin.

The woman lifted her head and scoured her fisted hands across bleary eyes. "Come back to bed, milord. I'm cold."

He caught her reflection in the shaving mirror, but he doubted the hard points of her breasts were due to any draft. She wanted to rut again. Ordinarily, he wouldn't have minded obliging her, but the disturbing dream refused to be dismissed.

"I canna." He ended it there, for in truth, he couldn't recall her name. To make up for his memory lapse and early departure, he turned and flipped several coins upon the bed to show his appreciation. "I must away and fetch my brother home."

EWAN LAY IN THE BIG BED thinking of Brianna and watching the late-afternoon shadows creep across the wall. At one point, a spider joined them, dropping down from the bed canopy on its silken thread, stopping near enough to his face to make his nose itch.

He turned to the cat once more curled upon the cushion next to him. The animal had reclaimed his perch shortly after his mistress so abruptly left.

"Go get it, boy."

The cat, Muffin, stared back at him and yawned. White around the muzzle and bleary of eye, he twisted about, tucked his head and began licking himself.

"You may be a graybeard, but at least you can still move freely." Ewan turned away, feeling almost jealous. Talking aloud to a cat was bad enough, but feeling jealous of one—what the devil had he come to?

The lowly spider could spin and the cat could bathe. It seemed everyone was at liberty to go about their business but him. The tack he was taking with Brianna obviously wasn't working. After her boldness in bed the night before, he'd thought that his being bold in turn would win her, but that did not seem to be so. He wondered if the MacLeod laird might not be a romantic at heart.

Their night together had shown him one thing, however. Romantic or not, beneath her tight-lipped, solemn-eyed exterior, Brianna was a very sensual woman. If only he could find a way to coax her into letting his hands loose, he was certain he could win his release.

There was a time not so very long ago when release would have been the very last thing on his mind. Chains notwithstanding, he would have given an eyetooth to find himself in her bed. Brianna MacLeod had haunted his dreams for ten years. He'd never entirely given up the hope that one day they might meet again, perhaps even wed.

Lying about, waiting for a beautiful redhead to rejoin you in bed, wasn't what most men his age would consider hard labor. His brother would like as not be in heaven now. Laird though he was, Callum was scarcely more industrious on an ordinary day. Ewan wondered when or even if his twin would bestir himself to send out a party to search. If Brianna were being honest about not holding him for ransom, she may not have sent any note.

He pushed the painful subject of his twin to the back of his mind and turned his thoughts back to Brianna. Whatever had befallen the bright-eyed girl she once had been? The woman he'd met again the other day remained very much a stranger to him. There was no laughter in her, and beyond that, precious little joy. It was as if the lifeblood had been drained from her and the marrow sucked from her bones. What was left of her seemed a beautiful but vacant shell. Being laird in such troubled times would be a weighty responsibility for anyone, but he sensed that whatever troubled her went beyond the press of duty.

She mustn't have been married all that long. Still, she

must have loved her husband dearly. Why else would she swear vengeance not only on Ewan's brother, the supposed murderer, but on an entire clan? The thought prompted a sharp jolt of jealousy.

He stopped himself before going any further, reminding himself that Brianna MacLeod was not the sort of woman for whom he could afford to feel sympathy— or anything else. She fully intended to use him like a stallion to render stud service to a broodmare. Though he badly wanted children, he didn't want them *that* way.

He glanced again at the cat, who'd finally finished bathing. "Do you think she'll make good on her word to lengthen my chains at least?"

The cat stared back, noncommittal.

"I don't suppose I could presume upon you to scratch my nose?"

Again, that fixed, slanted stare.

Across the room, a fly buzzed through the half-cocked window. Hunter instincts at the ready despite his age, the cat leaped off the bed and darted across the room. The fly dived. Ears pinned and tail twitching, Muffin jumped up onto the table. He missed, front paws catching on the table's edge and scattering chess pieces to the room's four corners.

Brianna must be a chess player. Otherwise, why would she have the game sitting out? Chess was a game favored by those who prized intellect and strategy over base physical force. Intellect…strategy. Ewan felt a grin splitting his face, a grin so broad that his scabbed bottom lip broke open and began to bleed. It was worth it, though. He had his answer, and it had been staring him in the face all along. If not by pleasuring Brianna's body, perhaps he could gain his freedom by wooing her mind.

7

Week Two

BRIANNA KEPT AWAY from Ewan for the next week, though she made certain that the servants saw to his comfort. The latter included calling in the blacksmith to lengthen his chains so that he might attend to his personal needs and move freely about the room. When she discovered he could read, she had her precious volume of Geoffrey Chaucer's *Canterbury Tales* sent in to divert him.

She was surprised when, through one of the guards, she received Ewan's invitation to join him. The request sent her heart somersaulting. To stall it, she told herself he only meant to plead for his release. What other possible motive could he have for seeking out the company of a woman he plainly loathed? Still, her courses had ended, which meant it was time again to try for a bairn. She hoped the measures taken to make his captivity more bearable would lessen his resentment. That he'd invited her to visit seemed a promising first step in that direction. Who knew but mayhap she might even find him willing, or at least not averse, to lying with her?

She found him sitting on the edge of the bed, the open volume of Chaucer's tales balanced between his broad hands, the lengthened chains from his manacled wrists pooling to the floor like twin serpents twining about his feet. Late-morning light streamed through the open window, and the fingers of a sea-scented breeze ruffled his shirtsleeves and dark hair.

She ran her gaze over his face. The worst of his cuts and bruises had faded, the gash on his forehead healed to a hairline-fine scab and the dark purple bruise riding his left cheekbone faded to pale yellow. For the first time she could properly appreciate how utterly handsome he was, how entirely grand. No longer swollen, his features were so perfectly formed they might have been rendered with a master sculptor's mallet and chisel. The cleft cleaving his chin was the one tiny flaw in God's grand plan. Struck by that beguiling indentation, Brianna couldn't wait to kiss him *there,* just there.

On her order, clothes had been unpacked from her father's chest. Though Ewan was a good deal taller and leaner than her father had been, still the saffron shirt with embroidered collar and cuffs, jerkin vest with pewter buttons and slim-fitting, fawn-colored trousers looked well on him. Privately, she'd wondered how the sight of him in her father's clothes might affect her, but to her pleasant surprise, it didn't bother her as she'd feared. Ewan's force-of-nature presence transformed the familiar garments into those uniquely his own.

As if sensing her there, he looked up. Their gazes connected and an instant later he flashed a welcoming smile. Basking in the unexpected warmth, Brianna let the door fall closed behind her, and approached.

"How do you fare this fine day, my lord?" Mindful of Milread and Alys's advice, she took care to lighten her tone.

His smile broadened into a grin, the brilliance reaching his eyes, which looked clear as crystal today, not shadowed. He must be feeling better indeed.

"I fare far better for the boon of this fine book. Thank you." He closed the volume with reverence, set it down on the bedside chest and rose.

He ran his gaze over her, a slow, measured assessment that had her cheeks heating. Mayhap it was only wishful thinking on her part, but she fancied she saw a glimmer of appreciation in his eyes when he lifted them to her face.

She trusted she looked well, if not precisely pretty. Alys had dressed her hair in a simple but flattering style, plaiting the front and then pinning the plaits to make a coronet about her crown. The rest was left loose, the long curls brushing her hips. Freshly washed that morning, the red-gold tresses had been dried in the sunshine and then brushed to a high sheen.

In addition to hairdressing, Alys had shown herself to be a nimble-fingered needlewoman. She'd altered Brianna's second gown for a closer fit. The scooped bodice accentuated the high slopes of her breasts, attributes she usually took pains to hide, and the yoked waistline showed off the slenderness of her torso and the subtle flare of her hips.

"And you, milady? How do you fare?" The warmth welling in his eyes told her he found her fine, indeed.

"I am well, thank you." Flustered, she fingered the chain about her throat and avoided looking into his eyes. Loath to face him the other night, she'd waited until he'd slept then crept in and retrieved her ring. It felt good to have it back.

A void of silence descended. Nervous with the need to fill it, she added, "Had I known you could read, I would have offered the book ere now."

He took a step toward her, his floor-length chains fording a path through the rushes and setting off firefly sparks from striking against the slate flagging. A quick glimpse about the chamber's four corners showed that he'd lost no time in availing himself of the new freedom—the basin of soapy water on the washstand, the unmade bed behind him, the second pillow still bearing the imprint of his head. Glancing to the dressing table, she saw that the chased silver hairbrush rested on its back, his black hairs threading through the bristles along with her red ones. The sight brought about a funny thickening in her throat.

"There is much you have yet to discover about me." His moonstone gaze fixed on her face, and his unblinking regard had her forgetting to breathe. "I am not such a savage as you might think."

God's blood, it seemed that in giving what was meant to be a compliment she'd somehow managed to offend him—again. Exasperated, she twisted her hands behind her back. "I did not think you were…oh, never mind. How do you find it?"

"Milady?" His puzzled gaze met hers.

"The book," she clarified, feeling near wit's end.

She didn't remember having such difficulty communicating with Donald, but then she and her husband had been raised almost as siblings. His countenance, while pleasing, had never tangled her tongue nor stolen her breath nor caused her otherwise stalwart limbs to wobble. And yet one glance from Ewan Fraser sufficed to do all of those things.

He tossed a backward glance over one broad shoulder to the book he'd set aside. "'The Wife of Bath's Tale' strikes me as particularly droll."

Brianna had had a similar reaction when she'd first opened the volume. She'd been a maid still and blissfully ignorant of how badly a marriage might go and the ribald antics of the merry widow had kept her in stitches. Older and if not wiser, certainly more jaded, Brianna did not feel much moved to laughter now. Though she'd had only one husband to the fictional widow's five, the parallel to her own life wasn't lost on her. Lest Ewan's thoughts wander along a similar path, she looked sharply away.

Her gaze alighted on her father's chessboard set out on the low, round-topped table. The carved alabaster pieces had come all the way from France. Though she hadn't anticipated playing anytime soon, she hadn't yet been able to bring herself to pack the game away. A quick glance confirmed an equal number of chessmen on both sides of the board had been moved.

She wandered over to the table. "You're full of surprises, Ewan Fraser. Not only do you read, but you apparently also play chess—albeit against yourself. That must present quite a challenge."

The clanking of chains announced he'd followed her. "Aye, it does, but then there are some…amusements that require a partner to be truly satisfying, even if that partner is an opponent."

Brianna's head shot up from the board she'd been pretending to study. It was clear from his expression he wasn't only speaking of chess. Her heart turned over. Heat flooded her lower belly. The sensitive spot between her thighs tingled and tightened.

Dark brows lifted, his regard holding steady beneath. "Do you play?"

She trailed her fingers over the curved chair back. The smooth, sun-warmed wood felt very much like the silken flesh stretched over Ewan's ribs. "Aye, my father taught me. Many a winter's eve we sat up late in this chamber with our heads bent over the board."

Those late-night sessions had more to do with preparing Brianna for her future as laird than any chess match. As The MacLeod, her charge would be to uphold the clan motto and hold fast—to her principles even when others cast aside theirs, to doing the right thing and not the easy thing, to being ever mindful that her duty was to the clan first and to her own desires last.

That meant setting aside her lovely fair-day memory and moving forth with the marriage to Donald. Her cousin had hailed from among her mother's kinfolk, the McBrides. With Beatrice dead, a marriage betwixt members of the next generation was needed to maintain the blood bond with the larger, more powerful clan. Crystal clear eyes, a quirky, kissable mouth and raven tresses that curled about a shirt collar made for a bonny memory, but a laird's marriage must be as carefully, as strategically mapped as a chess match.

"Are you any good?"

Jarred back to the present, Brianna snapped up her head. "Aye, I'm good. I bested my father a time or two, though only toward the end." Even when Magnus's strength had ebbed to that of a feeble old man, he'd insisted on being propped upon pillows in his chair rather than take to his bed.

"I'm said to be a fair player myself. Think you can best me?" The lopsided grin Evan lanced her lent him a delightfully roguish look.

She swallowed against the sudden dryness coating the inside of her mouth and forced her attention back to the board. "I canna say, milord, as I've no had the honor to witness your play, though I canna think why you would leave your bishop in so vulnerable a spot." She lifted her gaze to his, and it was as if sparks shot across the room.

"Can you not?" He stepped behind her, so close that one chain lightly slapped her backside. Brianna started, thinking he must mean some mischief, but instead he drew out one of two short chairs flanking the table and gestured for her to sit. "In that case, milady, consider yourself challenged—and your match met."

EWAN LOOKED UP from the rook he'd just moved. They'd been playing for nearly an hour, and a victor had yet to emerge.

"These clothes were your father's, aye?" He glanced down at his shirtsleeve.

The question took Brianna aback. She pulled her attention away from the move she'd been contemplating and looked up. "Aye, they are—were. But how did you know?"

The clothing might just as easily have belonged to her husband. She'd packed Donald's possessions off to the almshouse not long after he'd passed.

Ewan stretched out his arm to examine the embroidered cuff. "The stitch work is the same I've seen on your coat of arms in the great hall, the same on that bonny broach you wear." He pointed to the clasp pinning the plaid over her left breast, his finger hovering a hairsbreadth away from touching her. Her nipples swelled beneath her lacings and shift in response. "The beastie depicted is a bull, is it not?"

Brianna nodded and drew a deep, jagged breath. If only the fresh air wafting through the open window might clear her head of her groundless hopes and senseless fantasies.

"Malcolm was the third MacLeod laird, and bold warrior that he was, he was a wee bit overfond of the women and the drink. According to the story, he was at the wedding feast of a kinsman when he encountered the lovely lady wife of the Fraser laird. They fell in love, or at least she did, and began meeting in secret when the lady's husband was called away. One night Malcolm was riding home from their tryst, and he crossed paths with a fierce, mad bull. The beast charged and—"

"Your clan motif is based on cuckold's horns," Ewan interrupted.

Brianna blushed. "Well, that is one way of looking at it."

"I'm assuming Malcolm won out, otherwise there'd be no Brianna MacLeod to plague me?" His tone was teasing.

"Well, he slew the bull and not the other way 'round, if that's what you mean. I have the horns wrapped in cotton wool and stored in a trunk in my mother's old solar. We bring them out every so often for feast days and the like. I'll show you sometime if you wish." The latter implied he would be staying for a while.

Rather than commit to a yea or a nay, he asked, "What happened after?"

"After?" As far as she knew, the story ended there.

"Aye, the bull was slain, but was the lady loved?" His gaze snared hers.

Like an insect trapped in the sticky resin that would solidify into amber, she found herself caught up in the crystal clarity of his eyes. It took him clearing his throat to remind her that he was expecting an answer.

"The story does not say. I expect she remained with her husband. It was a dalliance only." The latter remark had Brianna looking away and heartily regretting having started down this bramble-riddled path.

"A dalliance?" He pondered that for a good long while. At length, he said, "So practical minded and serious you've become, milady. I canna help but wonder whatever happened to that braw, bright-eyed lassie I met on fair day ten years ago?"

It was her turn to move, but whatever strategy she'd plotted was lost to her now. She shook her head, feeling world-weary and more than a little old. "Ten years is a long time. Circumstances change. People change. When you are older, you will understand."

His eyes narrowed. "Dinna patronize me, Brianna. I

am your junior by two years only, and man enough to match you in all ways, not only in chess."

The boast wasn't lost on Brianna. She'd hoped to use this time to come to know him better, to rebuild their fledgling friendship from all those years ago, but it seemed that was not to be.

"I have no wish to quarrel with you, Ewan, and in truth, I did not come here to play chess." Her gaze strayed beyond him to the bed.

Looking more curious than angry, he asked, "Tell me, lady, why is it you've kept away from me all the past week? Is dallying with a chained man no to your liking after all?"

Heat climbed Brianna's cheeks. These unseemly blushes of hers really must cease. With the humiliations heaping one atop the other, she should be numb to embarrassment ere now. She wasn't. There was something about being around Ewan Fraser that made her feel young and vulnerable again, no longer a seasoned widow but a trembling, tenderhearted maid.

Still, she did her best to brazen it out. "Have you so little knowledge of a woman's body, Ewan Fraser, that you canna fathom the answer to that?"

Her secret hope had been to embarrass him, but judging by his jaunty expression, she'd failed in this, too. He slid his gaze boldly over her, a slow, languid sweep that set her heart aflutter and made her thankful she'd taken time to polish and rinse her teeth as well as suffer through Alys arranging her hair in a more becoming style.

His mouth remained impassive, neither smiling nor

scowling, but his eyes burned. "Unfetter my hands, lady, and I'll gladly show you just how well I ken the terrain."

Try as she might, there was no ignoring the sensual sorcery blazing from those beautiful gray eyes. Caught up in the spell of it, she felt warmth settling into her nether parts, making her uncomfortably aware of the narrowness of the little table between them.

Hold fast!

Snapping back to sanity, she reminded herself it wasn't pleasure that had steered her here, but duty. If she allowed her desires to enslave her, she had scant chance of putting Milread and Alys's advice into practice.

Resolved, she shook her head. "Had you free use of your hands, I ken you'd as soon wrap them about my throat as anything else."

His gaze never wavered. "You trusted me well enough ten years ago to turn over your wee knife. I gave it back, mind, and let you leave the stable at your da's beckoning. I might just as easily have covered your mouth with my hand and bore you down upon the straw. Virgin though I was, I spent the weeks after berating myself for letting you go with merely a kiss to remember me."

She swallowed hard, not only recalling the episode but *feeling* it all again—the excitement, the vulnerability, the yearning. Achingly young though they both had been, she didn't doubt they would have discovered what to do.

Her throat felt as dry as sawdust, her sex anything but. "My father was just outside." She wetted her lips, alarmed to hear her voice shake. "Had he found us, he would have killed you and locked me in a convent for the rest of my days."

Ewan didn't deny it. "I canna speak to the convent part, but it might have been worth it to die with the taste of Brianna MacLeod upon my lips."

As much as she resolved to remain unmoved, his hot-eyed gaze holding hers had her forgetting to breathe. "You're a devil, Ewan Fraser, with the serpent's tongue to prove it."

He lanced a wicked, knowing look her way, one corner of his mouth kicking up into the lopsided, devil-may-care grin she remembered from when he was a boy. "It's a canny clever tongue I have, and the wherewithal to use it." His expression sobered. "I'm a good lover, Brianna. I havena been with all that many women, but of the lassies who've gifted me their favors, nary a one has complained."

Brianna found herself at a loss for words but not for feeling. Jealousy flooded her, accompanied by a powerful, piercing hatred for the other women to whom he'd given himself freely.

He pushed back his chair and rose. "Ah, Brie, so it's come to this, has it?"

Before she might ask his meaning, he rounded the table to her side. Stepping behind her chair, he rested his chained hands heavily on her shoulders and leaned down. His warm spicy breath struck the side of her face. He'd been chewing fennel seeds, she could tell.

"If my giving you a bairn is the price of my freedom, then at least arrange matters so that we both might enjoy the act. Unchain me, Brie, and give me leave to show you the pleasure freed hands may bring."

Shivering beneath the shadow of all that masculine strength, Brianna shook her head. "I canna."

He slid his palms down her upper arms, pulling her back against the chair. "Canna or willna?"

Heat pooled in her lower belly; moisture blanketed her inner thighs. At her core, a liquid ache thrummed. Locking her knees, she swallowed hard, resolved not to let him see how her longing enslaved her. "They are one and the same."

"I think not." Pinning her left arm to the chair with one hand, he stroked his other over her swelling breasts and fluttering belly. Digits pointed downward, he stopped at the ring of keys tied to her kirtle. Playing his fingers over her lap, he whispered, "Tell me which of these wee keys is the one that unlocks these chains. Or on second thought, shall I try them all until I find the fit?"

She angled her face to look up at him. "You don't really think I'd be foolish enough to carry that key upon my person, do you?"

She was bluffing and they both knew it. One of those keys did indeed fit his manacles, though he'd have to go through nearly fifty before finding it.

As if reading her mind, he fitted his mouth to the shell of her ear. "You might as well unchain me. Fettered or no, were I so inclined, I could use my bare hands or these chains to snap that sleek neck of yours. Do you doubt it, Brie?"

Fear frissoned through Brianna. At the same time, she knew a powerful, primal thrill. Even though she was no lightweight or weakling, he already overpowered her with no effort at all. And suddenly she realized that Ewan's using his superior strength to overwhelm her wasn't something she feared. It was something she desperately wanted.

Hold fast, or so her clan motto prescribed. Seduce him into willingly spilling his seed inside her. Once it took root in her womb, send him on his way. End the feud between their clans and move forward with her future. It was a fine plan worthy of holding fast to, or so it had seemed—until now.

Resolved to ride out the madness, she held fast. "Mind, one shout from me would bring the guard bolting straight through yonder door."

"Aye, 'tis true, and yet to do so would spoil our game." Ewan angled his head and trailed warm, wet, openmouthed kisses to the juncture of her throat and bared shoulder. His teeth nipped at the chain about her throat. "What lies at the end of this?"

"The laird's seal ring. My ring." Swept up in sensation, she couldn't seem to dissemble.

"Take it off."

She swallowed hard and shook her head. "It's no meant to leave the laird's sight or person."

She'd been careless enough of late. The unfinished letter to Callum Fraser had not only slipped her mind, but apparently slipped through her fingers, as well. When she'd gone back to retrieve the ring, the letter hadn't been with it. She could have sworn she'd tucked it inside her writing desk before going below to preside over the court session. Then again, the news of Ewan's arrival had made such a coil of her thoughts it was hard to say.

His fingers played about her collarbone; his other hand

pressed hard into her shoulder. "I dinna want to make love to a laird. I want to make love to a woman—to you."

Ewan wanted her! Could it possibly be true? She swiveled her head to stare up at him. Ruse or truth, she should demand he release her. If he refused, she should make good on her threat to call out to the guard. She did neither. Instead, she sat still and melted like beeswax beneath the heat of his gaze, giving herself over to his rough hands and pillaging mouth, her sex weeping to take him inside her in every way, *any* way, she could.

He reached down to palm her, raising more of that lovely, thrumming heat. "I could try and escape." His words were a hot hiss in her ear, his hand massaging her mons an unholy torment from which she had no will to break free. "With my chain wrapped about their laird's slender white throat, I dinna think many a man would find the balls to try and stop me. I could take you as my hostage and carry you back to my castle and chain you to my bed as you have done to me. Only a pox on you, Brie, I want to lie with you more than I want to leave you. But I want to take you as a man this time, not as a chained beast."

A heartbeat later, she found herself hauled to her feet, the chair crashing to the floor. His erection bit into her backside; his arm took possession of her waist. He braced the edge of his other arm across her windpipe and bent down to kiss her, claiming the side of her neck with blood-warmed tongue and lips and teeth.

"Ah, Brie, admit it, you're wet for me already, are you not? Were I to lift your skirts, I'd find you dripping, aye?"

He didn't seem to expect or need her answer. He slid

his hand from her throat to between her thighs. Brianna widened her stance without his asking, silently begging for the pleasure that only he could bring.

She'd expected the lovely stroking to resume, but instead he grabbed her skirts and brought them up to her waist. Confronted with the copper-colored triangle of her bared sex, she let out a shocked cry. She tried yanking down her gown, but it was no use. He held her fast.

She struggled anyway. She tried biting his hand, and when that didn't work, kicked back, but to no avail.

His sharp laughter sounded in her ear. "Ah, Brie, you have the heart of a lion for all that you're a woman."

He shoved a hand between her legs. With his other hand, he drew one shackle across her sex and between her buttocks, pulling up hard in back until there was no slack and it fit as closely as a chastity belt.

Brianna froze. Cold metal grazed her sensitized flesh. Fury flared, coupled with heart-pounding, primal excitement. She twisted her head to look up at him. "Take your bloody hands off me."

His expression grim, he shook his head. "Nay more orders from you, milady laird." He gave the chain a sharp yank, grazing her vulva and buttocks at once. "If I must pay for my weakness, Brie, then so must you." He leaned in and claimed her mouth in a hard kiss.

8

EWAN BACKED BRIANNA across the room to the bed. Even
as he did so, he told himself he should be using this opportunity to escape, not make love. But instead of
putting time and distance between himself and his beautiful enemy, he couldn't seem to draw her close enough.

They came up on the bed. Hands on her shoulders,
he pushed her back across the mussed sheet. Hobbled
as she was, with the chain drawn taut between her
thighs, she had no choice but to go. He followed,
coming down atop her. Straddling her, he hauled her
arms over her head, banding both her wrists with one
hand. With his other, he kept firm hold on the chain as
he might a beast's leash, drawing a low moan from her
and forcing her to spread her legs wider.

He gazed down to the shackle grazing her sex, the
links squeezing the rosy swirls into two near perfect
halves. She was shiny wet and she smelled like heaven.

He reached down and smeared his fingertips with her
musky sweet dew. "How does it feel, Brie, to change
places with me?"

She didn't answer, but her body spoke for her, the
hard points of her nipples showing through her thin

woolen gown and desire leaking down her spread legs. He lowered his head and fitted his mouth over the tip of one breast. Wetting the fabric, he swirled his tongue over the taut bud.

"You're a knave, Ewan Fraser. I curse the day we met. I—" Her voice broke off on a shiver, her tented knees cinching his sides.

Ewan smiled against her breast. She wanted him.

As he did her. He'd been hard since he'd first looked up from the borrowed book to find her watching. During the chess match, he'd scarcely been able to attend to his next move for wondering what her body looked like beneath her clothes.

He vowed to find out.

He let the chain lie slack between her legs and tugged on the laces fronting her gown. A knife would have sliced cleanly through, but her men had disarmed him during his capture. He made do with his hands, yanking and tugging, reveling in the primal thrill that came of pretending he was ravishing her. Her wide eyes, arched spine and open legs assured him that whatever happened between them was as much her will as his.

The last lace frayed and then snapped. He pulled the halves of her gown apart and started on her shift. Unlike the heavy gown, the undergarment was made of a fine material. Taking hold of the smocked neckline, he ripped it open, pushed the ends aside along with the seal ring and took her breasts between his hands. Bringing the firm lobes tightly together, he suckled one rosy tip and then the other.

He drew back to look into her eyes, heavy lidded and

darkened with desire as though she'd been drugged. "You have bonny breasts, full and round and crowned with lovely long nipples. I've scarcely touched you and mark how they stand out, hard as pebbles." Ravenous, he bent his head and pillaged the tender flesh, loving how she moaned and thrashed beneath him, pleading with him to stop and then never to stop. He settled on tormenting her with his tongue, capturing each bud between his teeth and biting just hard enough to hurt. At the same time, he reached down and worked the chain between her legs, back and forth, side to side, again and again.

Brianna moaned and shifted beneath him. "Ewan, please, not like this."

He tore his mouth from her breast and met her pleading eyes. "Ah, don't tell me my lady laird hides a minstrel's soul beneath that steely strength of will. Spread your legs wide for me, Brianna. I mean to give you exactly what you crave and more."

Rocking back on his heels, he stared at her. Her gown was bunched at her waist, the bodice torn in half. Bright red hair spilled over the pillows and her mouth looked both swollen and moist. The lips of her sex were swollen, too, cream leaking from her chained slit and sliding down her thighs. Lying thus, wearing only the remnants of her clothes, she looked like a ravished Amazon princess, or better yet, Boadicea, a warrior queen enchained, yet not brought to heel.

Entranced, he pushed the chain to one side and thrust two digits deep inside her. Brianna gasped and tried wriggling away, but the shackle and his weight pinned her. He slid his fingers back and forth, her fluttering flesh soft as velvet and scalding as a brazier.

The scent of her drifted up to him. A cross between tangy salt air and freshly scythed hay, it made his mouth water and his cock throb. "Look at you, Brie. You're so wet one might think I'd spent the night wooing you with poetry and soft words."

His sharp laugh knifed through the quiet. He scarcely recognized it as his own. For good or for ill, Brianna MacLeod brought out the beast in him.

Her expression softened, the steel leaving her gaze. She looked as though she might cry. "Ewan, please…"

He felt a stab of annoyance at the sudden rush of guilt her pleading brought on. A merciful God would grant him the peace of loathing her. Not so, it seemed. Furious with her though he was, he couldn't fathom either hating or harming her.

"And why should I please you, Brianna? My end of our bargain is to give you a child and only that."

It was true. Beyond his ability to give her pleasure for the present and a child for the future, he was nothing and no one to her, not even a friend. Resolved to be ruthless, he slid two fingers beneath the chain, taking up the slack with a sharp twist. Brianna's eyes flew open.

She sucked in her breath. "Ewan, please, no more."

"Nay, Brie, it's more I'll give you, not only because you can take it but because you want it."

And she did want it. Her hitching breaths and hardened nipples and widespread legs gave lie to her pleading. He gave her more, moving the chain back and forth, gradually increasing the pace, the friction. Moisture spurted out of her, streaking down her thighs and melting into the mattress like snow. A vanquished moan broke from her parted lips. A moment later, she came apart in his hand, hips rocking, perspiration pearling on her forehead and breasts.

Ewan stared at his glistening fingers and drenched palm and allowed that he wasn't done with her, not nearly. Sliding down until he was eye level with her sex, he stroked his tongue upward from slick slit to hard clitoris, licking his way around the metal links. Tonguing her tangy folds, he felt his own member swell to bursting, his balls tight and aching. Resolved though he was to break that damnable iron will of hers, he felt as though his own will danced on the head of a pin.

He pleasured her with his mouth, bringing her to the cusp of a second climax. Instead of seeing it through, he sat up and grabbed hold of her wrists, forcing her arms above her head once more.

He fixed his gaze on her face and savored the sound of her whimper. "I could hurt you if I chose. As it is, you'll likely have bruises on the morrow. Once I let you up, what punishment will you mete out? Will you have me starved, whipped, thrown into your dungeon and broken on the rack? Not too broken, though. You have need of my cock for a while yet." He dragged his hardness along the inside of her thigh, as he'd dragged the fetter before. As badly as he ached to enter her, he desperately needed to hear her beg first. "Admit you want more from me than a dalliance or even a baby."

Tears welled in her eyes. Her lower lip trembled. "I admit nothing."

He gave her fettered hands a shake. "Admit I mean something to you, something more than a stiff cock between your legs."

She thrashed her head back and forth on the pillow. "Nay, I willna."

He reached down between them and tugged on the chain, the links between her legs coated with her cream so that it slid as if oiled.

"Admit you've dreamed of me all these many years, as I've dreamed of you. Admit that nights when you're alone, you spread your legs and finger that sweet spot between your thighs and pray to God for a chance to lie with me. Admit you want me now, even after my hands have left bruises and my mouth marks. Admit you want me more than ever and not only to get a child. Admit you want me for myself, just as I want you, Brie."

She stared up at him. "You want me?" A tear squeezed out of the corner of her eye and disappeared into her hairline, followed by another and another still.

He hesitated. In pushing her to confess, he'd said far more than he'd meant to, and yet he couldn't find it in him to regret it. It was no great secret. He wanted her and always had.

"Aye, I do."

Brianna wetted her lips. Her moist eyes met his. "I want you, too, Ewan. I have since first we met."

Ewan's heart wrenched. Mere moments before he'd wanted to bend her to his will. More than bend her, he'd wanted to humiliate and break her. Now that he had, all he wanted was the chance to set to rights everything that had gone so terribly wrong between them.

Tenderness rushed through him. He let go of the chain between her legs and trailed his fingertips along her tear-striped cheek, the scent of her hovering on his hands like a phantom glove, the tang of her staying on his lips and tongue like an exotic spice.

"Then make love with me, Brie. Not to me but with me. Not because it's your duty to beget a baby and end a feud, but because you want to, because you want *me*."

HOURS LATER THEY LAY side by side in the bed, exhausted, sated, and for the moment, wholly at peace. Sunlight streamed through the lead glass windowpanes, bathing them in gentle golden light. Like a slain dragon, the chains lay on the floor, and with them the manacles. The key had indeed been among those in Brianna's possession, though it had taken several patient tries to locate the exact one. The look of relief on Ewan's face when the manacles fell away had made her want to weep and laugh in equal measure.

Turning onto her side, Brianna tucked her hands beneath her head and regarded the clean lines of his profile with a loving eye. She had lusted after Ewan Fraser since she was fourteen years old. Beyond their physical attraction, she'd felt a kinship, a soul-deep connection from the very start. He wasn't the only one of them to regret her leaving that stable with only a kiss. Were she gifted with the chance to travel back ten years, she had no doubt that this time she would stay. If her father found them together, then so be it. She would have asked for no greater honor than to be Ewan Fraser's handfast bride.

But that choice had not been hers to make, and in the end, she had married Donald as decreed. Ewan, however, had never wed. For a man in his position to reach the age of two and twenty and remain single stood out as a most unusual state.

The reason struck her with the suddenness of a summer storm. "You waited for me, didn't you? All these years, you waited."

He stared up at the canopy. Other than a muscle ticking in his jaw, his face was expressionless. "Does it matter? Would you release me if I told you I had a wife and bairns waiting at home?"

Heart thudding, she asked, "Do you?"

He shook his head. "Nay."

Brianna let out the breath she hadn't realized she'd held. "I'm glad," she admitted, and for now left it at that.

He turned his head to look at her. "Are you?"

Heart hitching, she reached for her courage. "Aye, verra glad."

As swiftly as the tide, he rolled atop her. With muscled arms braced on either side of her head, he said, "Then show me."

Show him. Brianna bit her lip. Before now she'd never thought of herself as a coward. Had never fled from a fight. The MacLeod motto enjoined clansmen to "hold fast." She had taken those words to heart all her life.

And yet the urge to leap up from the bed and run from the room threatened to overwhelm her. But if she did so, she wouldn't be running to something.

She would be running away.

Like generations of MacLeod ancestors, she must

stay the course. She must hold fast to her plan to transform Ewan into a willing lover. Even though he'd given her pleasure beyond her wildest imaginings, her most fervent dreams, so far she had been the only one of them to be satisfied. Ewan's hardness pressing into her lower belly suddenly seemed a silent reproach. Threads of Milread's and Alys's counsel filtered through the fog of her muddled mind, naughty bits designed to drive men mad with lust and longing.

Beyond begetting a baby, Brianna wanted to drive Ewan as mad as he had driven her.

She reached up and stroked her hand down the side of his face. Though he'd shaved that morning, already stubble shadowed his cheeks and jaw.

Grazing her fingertips on the sandpapery texture, she said, "I don't have a great deal of experience in these matters, but I'd like to try. Will you give me leave?"

Clear eyes bore into hers. He answered with a mute nod and drew away from her. Grateful when he didn't force an explanation—she was a widow, after all—she sat up and swung her legs over the bedside.

Her bare feet met the floor and, naked, she rose. Fighting her shyness, she slowly turned back around. "First let me make you more comfortable. Will you stand for me, please?"

Eyes wide, he rose and crossed to her side of the bed until he stood before her. Rather than reach for the tattered remains of her clothes or other covering, she focused on Ewan, not only his body but his eyes. Mindful of Alys's assertion that men fancied being teased, she took her time undressing him, beginning with his shirt, pretending she was unwrapping a present, reminding herself that in truth, she was.

She slid a hand inside his open shirt. Crisp hair teased her palm and fingertips, setting her skin to tingling. He sucked in a breath and covered her hand with his larger one.

"Ah, Brie."

His flesh felt fevered to the touch. Eager to see all of him, she pushed the shirt off his shoulders, revealing his powerful chest, the dusting of dark hair starting at his firm pectorals and narrowing into a queue that trailed downward over his taut belly and disappeared into his trousers. When she'd seen his naked body before it had been shrouded in evening shadow. Seeing him in full daylight, she was shocked by the extent of his wounds.

"Ah, Ewan, we have used you ill, have we not?"

Tall though she was, he topped her by several inches. She stretched up and brushed her lips over one shoulder, where a whip mark was healing, but still wickedly deep.

Ewan didn't answer. He swallowed hard and slid his hand beneath the fall of her hair, guiding her mouth to the flat brown disc of his nipple, sucking in a hard, heavy breath when she traced his areola with the tip of her tongue and then drew the teat between her teeth.

His groan filled the silence. "Och, lass, what witchery is it you're practicing upon me?"

A few days before, such a statement would have hurt her feelings. It *had* hurt her feelings. But now she understood that his likening her to a witch didn't mean he found her warty and old. He found her mysterious, alluring. Before the afternoon's end, she meant for him to find her irresistible.

Feeling equal parts feminine and powerful, she lifted her head and looked up into his taut features. "No witchery, milord. Only lovemaking arts."

Indeed, having started down this path, she found she couldn't wait to put into practice every salacious secret and tantalizing tidbit she'd learned from her two friends. Careful not to rush, she traced the waist of his trousers with a single finger and then began working the fastenings at the front, the fabric pulled taut by the bulge crowning his loins. Remembering the velvety slickness of his member moving inside her mouth made her sex moisten and thrum.

The trouser flap fell open. His erection surged forth, proud and free. Impatience seized Brianna. She slid the garment down his tapered hips and muscled thighs and calves and then took him in her hand.

According to Alys and Milread, give a man too much too soon and his desire waned. As on the battlefield, advance and retreat were the key elements of the game. Accordingly, she caught his eye and slid her tongue along her bottom lip, but held back from stroking him.

"Ah, Ewan, the scent and taste of you has filled my every dream and waking moment for a full week now."

It occurred to her that she had revealed too much, and yet with this man, she seemed to find it next to impossible to hold back. She sank to her knees. Furling her fingers about him, she bent her head and slowly slid him into her mouth, her tongue playing about the tip, her lips rimming him.

After suckling, she withdrew. Looking up into his

taut-featured face, she sighed. "Umm, lovely…even more savory than I remembered. Only I want more… much more." She angled her mouth to take him again. Relaxing her throat, she drew him deeper still.

Ewan's gasp filled the chamber. "So warm…so wet…so…bloody…good."

He threaded frantic fingers through her hair and thrust inside her. She sucked him greedily, and then teased him again by withdrawing, to flick her tongue over the tip of his shaft.

She stared up at him, summoning what she hoped were innocent eyes. "Tell me what you want."

"I want you to keep doing…*that*."

"This?" She took him into her mouth again, only slowly this time, teasingly, inch by inch.

Ewan's deep, guttural groan rose above her. He tried thrusting again, only this time Brianna held him at bay, determined to torture him with pleasure for as long as she could. Seconds merged into minutes and then time stilled altogether. Lost to the scent and taste and texture of him, she could have happily gone on until nightfall.

Not so Ewan. "Enough, Brie! I canna bear more, not now." Laying a hand on either side of her head, he urged her back.

He turned away to step out of his trousers, affording her a glorious view of broad, sculpted muscles, and taut buttocks she couldn't wait to bite into, to lick.

But that would come later. He laid his hands on her waist and sat down on the side of the bed, pulling her onto his lap.

"You know what I want, aye?" The glint in his eyes dared her to deny him.

Brianna nodded. "I think so."

She'd never before coupled in that way, yet sitting upright, astride a lover's lap and looking into his eyes while meeting him thrust for thrust, had long been a fantasy of hers. She complied, positioning her legs on either side of him.

His member stood out between them, the size and breadth of it stealing her breath. She hesitated and then braced her hands on his shoulders. He reached down between them and guided himself to her.

He settled the head of his cock into her slit, testing her slickness and teasing the bud topping her nether lips. Impatient, she wiggled, wanting him inside her.

"Ah, Brie." He ran his hands beneath her buttocks and thrust hard, burying himself to the base.

Stretched and filled to her limit, Brianna felt pleasure beyond her wildest imaginings. She anchored both hands to his shoulders, forgetting to be gentle, and lifted her hips to meet him as he began to move.

For Brianna, the outside world fell away. Reality became reduced to the slapping of damp flesh against damp flesh, to the moans filling the steamy air between them, and to the hot, hard press of Ewan inside her.

Her nails dug into his shoulders. She lifted herself and came down hard, the blunt pressure beautiful beyond words. In the throes of it, she confessed, "I don't just want a baby. I want *your* baby."

"Brie?"

Still joined, she pushed him backward on the bed and

came down atop him. "You heard me. I want you to give up your seed because I want your bairn in my belly. I want to feel myself increasing and know that the child I carry isna only mine but yours as well."

The admission opened a dark, locked place inside Brianna. Not only was her body fully opened to him but her heart was headed that way, too. Later she would ponder the danger of that, but for now she was beyond fear.

She tightened her knees about him and thrust hard. "I want your baby, Ewan, because I want you."

His eyes looking up into her face were feral, raw. He grabbed hold of her waist and pulled her down roughly, impaling her on his erection. "Oh, God, Brie."

Ewan pumped into her, the length and breadth of him reaching deep inside her. Warmth sprayed into her, triumph and pleasure rolling over her like a wave. Ewan Fraser hadn't just released his seed inside her. He had done so of his own free will.

Brianna's triumph was heady, her pleasure intense. Her inner flesh fluttered about him and she came yet again. A starburst of pleasure streaked through her, and she collapsed atop him, pliant and weak.

SOMETIME LATER, Ewan rose up on his elbow and stared down at her. "I want to taste you, milady. I want to suckle you as you have me."

Brianna toyed with the edge of the coverlet. "Didn't you, uh…kiss me there earlier?"

Smiling, he yanked the covers down. "Aye, but this time there'll be no chains, only my mouth on your sex."

He combed his fingers through her dewy curls. "Straddle my face, Brie."

"What?"

"You heard me well enough. Straddle my face and ride my mouth as though it were your saddle. Let me pleasure you. Let me pleasure us both, unless of course you are afraid." The latter held a hint of provocation.

"Are you challenging me, Ewan Fraser?" Brianna had never turned down a dare in her life.

Ewan shrugged. "Aye, I suppose I am."

She sat up. "In that case, I accept."

Grinning, he lay back down. Brianna threw one leg over and shimmied up the length of him. Hands braced on her hips, he urged her into position level with his mouth.

She had forgotten how broad his shoulders were. With her knees braced outside them, she felt like a wishbone on the verge of splitting. She was completely open to him, utterly wet. Even though he hadn't kissed her yet, she sensed she was very close to coming.

"Ah, Brie, what a feast for the senses you are." He touched her with the tip of his tongue, a butterfly-light stroke that had her gasping.

Before that afternoon, Brianna had never felt a man's mouth on her sex. Experiencing Ewan's stroking tongue and soft, intimate kisses was like floating toward heaven while an invisible cord still connected her to earth. She felt as though she'd left her body, and yet at the same time had never lived in it quite so fully. Her core throbbed with a building ache, her fingertips and toes tingled, her back arched and her buttocks lifted in anticipation of an even greater pleasure to come. Looking down at his dark head framed between her thighs, she realized she had never so thoroughly enjoyed, so utterly *savored*. The warmth welling in his eyes when he paused from pleasuring her told her he was pleasuring himself, as well. Ewan's lust for her was proving an aphrodisiac more potent than any charm or potion Milread might prescribe. More than the delicious sensations his laving lips and warm, circling tongue aroused, it was knowing that he desired her completely, wanted her fully, that drove her toward the brink.

In the midst of her building pleasure, tears pricked her eyes. With Donald she'd felt like an annoyance, a supplicant, and at times even a beggar. Surely her husband had never gifted her with so intimate and tender a kiss. What tepid pleasure he had given her had always come with a price. But Ewan wasn't granting her a boon or bartering for a favor. She didn't appear to be bothering him, taking him away from his beloved books or other favorite pursuits. He was enjoying making love to her. Though her body was too large in places and her responses to him more passionate than polished, he didn't seem to mind. He seemed to *like* making love to her, and was only too happy to take his time.

His hands fell away from her buttocks and drifted over the front of her. He spread her nether lips wide, a kind of wonder breaking over his face. "I've fantasized about how you might taste ever since we first met."

She'd been shy at first, but not so now. She bucked against his mouth, wound her hands about the headboard spindles and spread her thighs as far apart as they would go until she felt as though she might splinter. Perspiration filmed the backs of her knees, the delicious tingling climbing to a crescendo.

The climax broke over her like a storm, the contractions striking deep, their aftermath soul shattering. She felt the force in her whole body, her belly, back and buttocks, her fingers and feet. Past caring who might hear, she threw back her head and screamed. Her instinct was to pull away, but Ewan anchored his hands to her hips and pulled her closer, lapping her essence as though it was divine nectar of which he couldn't possibly sate himself.

Only when the last contraction ebbed did he permit her to climb off and settle beside him. Turning over on his side, he gathered her against him.

Mouth moist and eyes passion dark, he cocked a brow and stared at her. "Have I proved myself worthy, milady? Have I won your trust?"

Brianna nodded. Like a knight laying siege, he had breached the last of her defenses and claimed her for his own. He'd won her, not with poet's promises and languishing gazes, but with the force of his passion and also his caring. There was little she would refuse him now, absolutely nothing of herself she would withhold. Outside the chamber's four walls, she was the MacLeod laird, but within them she was Ewan Fraser's woman.

"Aye, milord, you have won that and more."

9

THE SUN WAS SINKING when Brianna left Ewan to return to her mother's chamber to bathe, a cloak concealing her rent clothing. Passing by the guard, Hugh this time, brought stinging heat into her cheeks. Solid though the chamber door was, he most surely had heard them.

She found Alys perched upon a tapestry-covered chair cushion, plying her needle and humming a soft tune beneath her breath. As always, the girl looked lovely, her golden hair braided and coiled at her nape, her head uncovered, as she was in the privacy of the chamber. Brianna had made certain that a gown was found to replace the old yellow one. The deep blue dress brought out her eyes and molded her small figure to perfection. Subtle modifications, including a smattering of smocking at the sleeves, showed Alys had used her idle time to good result. Sitting thus in domestic tableau, she looked more like a knight's lady than a maid.

She set her needlework aside and rose, dipping into a low curtsy. Rising, she eyed Brianna strangely. "Milady, is it cold outside?"

Brianna hesitated and then realized Alys must be

wondering why she wore a winter cloak. Heat stung her cheeks. Not yet willing to admit just how well the advice had worked, she put off answering and instead asked, "Where is Alasdair?"

The maid's expression softened into a smile. "He has a tooth coming in. It is making him fussy. I tried rubbing his gums with a wee bit of whiskey, but still he cries. Milread is keeping him for me."

Brianna braced herself for the familiar stab that struck whenever the subject of babies arose, only to find that the sensation seemed to have dropped off to a minor twinge. She wouldn't have thought it possible even a fortnight before, but she must be moving beyond her grief. Her time with Ewan Fraser was proving to be healing in more ways than one.

Alys stepped behind her mistress and reached up to remove the cloak. Biting her lip, Brianna let the garment slide off her. With the cloak draped over her slender forearm, Alys came forward. One look had her blue eyes growing wide. "Oh, my, are those…love bites upon your neck and…breasts?"

Holding the front of her gown together, Brianna nodded. "Aye, they are." The admission brought the heat simmering in her face to a full boil. Focusing her gaze across the room, she admitted, "You and Milread give most excellent advice."

Setting aside her reserve, Alys let out a very uncharacteristic whoop. Dancing on her toes, she looked up at Brianna, blue eyes beaming. "Milady, I am so happy for you."

"Thank you."

As if suddenly recalling her place, she ceased her prancing. "Shall I draw a bath for you?"

A full bath was no small feat. Water had to be brought in from the well, heated in the kitchen, and then copper-lined buckets carried up numerous flights of steep, winding stairs. Beyond being loath to put such a burden on Alys's slender shoulders, Brianna realized that for once she was in no haste to bathe. Bathing meant washing away Ewan's scent.

She glanced over to the washstand where, on her instructions, a basin of fresh water was set out, along with a clean cloth and a bar of Milread's special soap. "The water in yonder ewer will serve my needs, I think."

She sat down on the side of the bed that someone, Alys no doubt, had made that morning. When her maid remained standing, Brianna patted the space beside her. Growing up among boys as she had, she realized she missed having female friends.

She waited for Alys to seat herself and then asked, "By the by, how are you getting on?"

More than idle curiosity motivated the question. Fleeting though Brianna's bliss might be, still she couldn't help wishing Alys might find some happiness herself. It would be so lovely if some stalwart knight stepped forward to sweep the maid off her tiny feet.

The girl paused. "Everyone has been most kind. I helped in the dairy this morning. Tomorrow I'm promised to the cook at the noontime. I like the dairy work best, for it's what I know."

Brianna smiled. It wasn't the answer for which she'd been fishing, but then again, contentment came in many forms. "I would not have pegged you for a dairymaid." Delicate as a china doll, Alys hardly fit Brianna's mental image of a braw, strapping farm girl.

Alys's expression turned thoughtful. "I didn't always ply the trade, milady."

Brianna shook her head, sensing she might have given offense. "I did not suppose you did. I only meant that you do not much resemble most dairymaids I've seen. With your fair looks and gentle manners, you would not disgrace a nobleman's table."

The compliment, sincerely meant, had color rushing to the girl's pale cheeks. "That is very kind of you, milady, but in truth I grew up working my da's dairy in the Borders."

The other day in court Brianna thought she'd detected a Lowlands accent. Along with being a woman of the street, being a Lowlander would have made Alys doubly despised. Small wonder the burgher's widow had found it a simple matter to steal her child.

Now that the lid had been lifted off Pandora's box, Alys seemed in no hurry to close it again. "I lived there all my life until two years ago, when I met my husband."

"You were married?" Brianna couldn't quite keep the shock from her tone. She was beginning to see there was a good deal more to her maid than first met the eye.

Alys turned her pretty face to the side. "Aye, I was. Does that surprise you?"

Catching the canniness in the girl's quick glance, Brianna suspected it was pointless to dissemble. "A little. You are very young."

Alys looked down at her folded hands and sighed.

"My husband was a foot soldier in the English army. We met one day when one of my cows broke loose and I went to fetch her."

The other day in court Brianna had been too caught up with anticipating her reunion with Ewan to give the girl's background much thought, but now the details fell into place. "So you wed an Englishman?" It wasn't really a question.

She hesitated. "Aye. I named Alasdair after his da, only 'tis the Scots version, mind. My husband was Alexander." The worried, wild-eyed look returned, and the folded hands in her lap clenched. "I hope you willna reconsider your kindness and turn us out because of it."

"Of course not, Alys. Do not trouble yourself on that score. You and Alasdair have a home here for as long as you wish it."

Grateful tears filled the girl's eyes. "You have a good heart, milady. Not everyone does. My parents' disapproval was the reason Alex and I met in secret. When I discovered I was with child, we ran away and came north. Bribing the priest to marry us took the last of our coin. The month before Alasdair was born, Alex caught a fever and…died."

Brianna's heart ached. For the past months, she'd been so mired in her own troubles she'd forgotten others had theirs, as well. Considering how privileged she was compared to her maid, she felt guilty for having indulged in her unhappiness as long as she had.

She reached out and covered Alys's small folded hands with one of hers. Giving a light, reassuring squeeze, she said, "That's a verra sad tale indeed."

Alys shrugged as though such heartache was happenstance. "I hadn't kin to take us in or coin to get back home to my family, so we stayed on." Head tilted toward Brianna, she opened her rosebud mouth and then closed it again, as though deciding against saying more.

"If there is something you wish to say to me, Alys, pray feel free to do so. We are quite alone here, and I would have you think of me as a friend."

"Do you love him, milady?"

Brianna hesitated. Of all the questions Alys might have asked, she felt least prepared to answer that.

Weighing her words with care, she said, "Ewan Fraser is my sworn enemy. His brother murdered my late husband, and even before that our clans were feuding."

Alys leaned in, her gaze holding Brianna's. "But do you love *him*, milady?"

"Until the other week, we hadna seen each other for ten years. And then, we met only once on a fair day."

The maid's face took on a wistful look. "The moment I laid eyes upon my Alex, I knew in my soul he was the only one for me, nay matter that he was English and the enemy, or that my da would beat me within an inch of my life if he found us out. I just knew I loved him. Nay matter how badly things turned out later, I wouldn't trade a single moment of our short time together for all the world's riches."

To love and be loved like that in return, Brianna envied her. She and Donald had been friends in their youth, but once wed, there had been precious little passion between them. Once she'd discovered she was pregnant, their conjugal encounters had fallen off altogether. At the time she'd tried telling herself that soon she'd be too busy caring for their baby to fret over the nighttime neglect, but his disinterest had wounded her all the same.

Bedding Ewan had shown her just how much she had missed in her marriage. That he wasn't her lawful husband was mattering to her less and less. He was the perfect lover, the personification of her every secret wish and dark fantasy. As if reading her mood, he knew when she wanted to be taken slowly and gently or fast and hard. Shameful though it was to admit, remembering how he'd used his male strength to master her had her heart skipping beats and her sex strumming. As many times as they'd made love that day, already she wanted him again. Were they ever to marry, she had no doubt that he would continue finding new ways to surprise and delight her. Even though he would be free to go after she confirmed her pregnancy, like Alys with her Alex, Brianna couldn't bring herself to regret the time they'd shared.

She started up from the bed. "Thank you, Alys."

The girl lifted startled eyes. "For what, milady?"

"For sharing your story and your wisdom with me."

Alys blushed. "Whether we die as weans or live on to reach a great age, our earthly lives amount to little more than a teardrop in time. If we do not love one another truly and well whilst we are here, what then is the point of it all?"

Thinking of Ewan unchained, yet still locked in her turret chamber, Brianna found herself silently agreeing. What was the point, indeed?

CALLUM FRASER WAS NOT having a good day. His trek on horseback to Ewan's special place had turned up a cold campfire and his brother's boots. A man didn't simply walk off and leave his boots behind.

Callum dismounted and walked about the spot. When something crunched beneath his foot, he looked down with a frown to see it was his brother's sporran.

This wasn't looking good.

He knelt to pick up the pouch, cold fear lancing through him. As much as he might want to, he couldn't overlook the obvious.

Ewan had met with violence.

Who would wish to harm him? It simply made no sense. Gentle, kind and, well, *noble,* his twin had no enemies to speak of, at least none Callum knew of. He, on the other hand, had made more than his share, mostly cast-off mistresses threatening to cut off his balls, and their furious fathers or brothers, swearing that, laird or no, they would run him through. Recently it had reached his ears that the new MacLeod was blaming him for her husband's murder. As accusations ran, that was particularly daft. To his knowledge, he had never touched shadows with her husband, let alone come close to killing him.

A rider rode up, interrupting his reverie. The man dismounted and sketched a brief bow. "My laird, forgive me for disturbing you, but this arrived after you set out."

Heart drumming, Callum reached for the message. Even though he'd felt no physical sign of it as yet, the thought occurred to him that Ewan might be dead. Callum broke the wax seal and unfolded the parchment. Bending his head to read, he felt sweat break out all over his body.

"I have taken your brother as you took my husband.
An eye for an eye…
Brianna, Chief of the MacLeods"

Callum crushed the missive with his fist. Whatever The MacLeod wanted of him, it didn't sound as though she meant to extract the ransom in cattle or gold. Sitting back in the saddle, he marshaled his fury. Absorbing the message, he realized something struck him as off. The first two lines were most definitely penned by a woman, but the signature was larger, ungainly. And the sundry ink blotches and cross-hatchings hinted at a hesitancy not commonly found among leaders. But there was no denying the wax impression with its bull's head and motto in Latin had been made by The MacLeod's own seal. He'd seen messages marked with that very same seal when he and Ewan were boys.

"News of Lord Ewan, milord?"

Callum looked over to the messenger, searching his face. His asking was a breach of protocol, but one that, under the circumstances, Callum was willing to forgive. Ewan was the perennial favorite among his fellow clansmen and always had been.

Callum nodded. "Aye, it seems The MacLeod has seen fit to abduct him, though I dinna ken why. Nay matter. Ride back to the castle and muster our forces. I want our best men dispatched to march on the morrow."

SEVERAL DAYS LATER, Brianna sat on the garden bench, twisting a daisy in her hand and plucking off the petals in turn.

He loves me, he loves me not, he loves me....

She gazed across the garden to where Alasdair and Alys played patty-cake on the grass. Being around babies no longer bothered Brianna as it had just a few weeks ago. If anything, she found she enjoyed it. Since her talk with Alys the day before, the girl's heartfelt question had remained uppermost in her thoughts. *Do you love him, milady?*

Afterward, she'd sponged herself clean and then laid down for a much-needed nap. Refreshed, she'd awakened in time to sup with Ewan in her solar. Spending time together without chains between them had added a new intimacy to the meal. Later, he'd made love to her very slowly and very gently. She'd ended the evening by falling asleep in his arms. What bliss!

Happiness was rendering her addled, though. Mislaying personal items had become a habit of late. The other day, she'd lost track of her seal ring yet again. Since sleeping with Ewan, she'd gotten into the habit of taking off the necklace at night and setting it aside, in her desk drawer. The other night she'd done just that before joining him in bed.

Yet the next day, when she'd remembered, and returned to fetch the ring, it was nowhere to be found. Now that she was laird, there were so many people in and out of her chamber it was hard to keep track. She hated to think there was a thief in their midst, but after an hour of scouring the place and coming up empty-handed, it seemed the obvious conclusion. Finally, in desperation, she'd called in Alys to help her search. The girl had found the ring at the bottom of the drawer where Brianna always left it.

Might Alys have "borrowed" the ring and then seized on the chance to return it? Watching her playing with Alasdair, Brianna dismissed the unworthy thought. So far the maid had shown herself to be the soul of gratitude and loyalty. Besides, what use could she have for a seal ring? As jewelry went, it was hardly a fashionable piece. Still, it was all very odd. As much as Brianna had come to dislike wearing the heavy chain and ring to bed, she meant to do so from here on.

Duncan's striding through the lych-gate interrupted her reverie. Halting before her, he bowed. Straightening, he appeared grave indeed.

"What brings you here, milord, on such a fine spring day?" Since Ewan's coming back into her life, all her senses felt particularly attuned.

Duncan refrained from commenting on the weather. He glanced down at the flower she held, all but two of its petals scattered at her feet, and scowled. "Your advisors seek an audience with you, milady, in the private council chamber."

Bracing for bad news, Brianna nodded. "Of course. But pray tell me, on what subject?"

He hesitated. Glancing over to Alys and the boy some distance away, he dropped his voice and added, "I am not at liberty to speak of it here, but trust me, the matter is of grave importance. Its consideration cannot be delayed."

Brianna fought a sinking sense of dread. She rose

from the bench. "Very well, then. Inform the gentlemen we shall meet at two in my private council chamber."

"As always, you are most generous." He bowed and turned to go.

Watching him stride up the path, Brianna felt unease settle in the pit of her stomach. She couldn't help thinking the session must have something to do with Ewan. Her hostage had become scarcely a prisoner at all, but rather an honored guest, a friend. Friend or not, who was it she strove to fool? Ewan wasn't only her guest or friend, though he was both those things. He was her lover and, she hoped, the father of her future child, a child she might carry already. If only she could make him her husband as well, how happy she would be. And yet so long as the blood feud continued, there was no hope of that. Her clansmen would never stand for a Fraser as their laird's consort. It was one thing for her to bear a baby that she might legitimize at a later time, but not even a laird was at liberty to recite marriage lines with the brother of her husband's murderer.

And yet her heart held on to the hope there might yet be a way.

She returned her attention to the flower. Two petals remained.

He loves me not. He loves me.

I love him not. I…love him.

The warmth in Ewan's gaze when he looked upon her and the gentleness in his touch when they made love now bespoke of a certain fondness. Whether or not he might come to love her in time she couldn't say, but she already more than loved him. Cupid's arrow had struck her heart ten years earlier and, as befit her clan motto, had indeed held fast.

Pitching the denuded flower aside, Brianna hurried from the garden to seek out Ewan.

EWAN SAT ON THE stone bench in the orchard reading *The Canterbury Tales,* or rather trying to. He'd moved on to "The Knight's Tale," and though he wasn't finding it as engrossing as the others, still it helped to pass the time. More and more of late, the hours spent apart from Brianna weighed heavily indeed. Given the blood feud, it wouldn't do for them to be seen together in public overmuch, though by now, every castle occupant between six and sixty surely knew they shared a bed.

He was surprised Callum hadn't come for him by now. Clearly, Brianna hadn't sent any ransom note. Instead of whiling away his time, Ewan should be planning his escape. One-on-one, the rat-faced guard would be easy to overtake. Only Ewan hadn't the heart. As much as he loathed being a captive, freedom meant saying goodbye to Brie.

For all he knew she might already be carrying his babe. But pregnant or not, laird or not, it scarcely mattered to him. He wanted her for herself alone. For the past hour, he'd racked his brain for a way to make Brie his bride, but so long as the blood feud raged, neither clan would sanction such a union. If he could clear Callum's name, they might have a chance at happiness—a slim one, but a chance all the same. No matter how damning the supposed evidence was, he couldn't see his twin as a murderer.

"Ewan."

The sound of Brianna calling to him caught him off guard. He nearly dropped the book on the damp ground. Catching it, he looked up. "Brianna…my lady, what brings you here?" Absurdly glad to see her, though they'd parted only an hour ago, he closed the book, set it on the seat and rose.

Rather than answer, she cast her gaze toward the guard, Seamus. He'd been lounging on the opposite bench, and must have seen her coming, because he'd jumped up and snapped to attention mere seconds ago.

"I would speak to Lord Ewan in private. You may leave us."

Seamus cut his gaze to Ewan and scowled. "But milady, Lord Duncan's orders are that I am not to let the prisoner out of my sight."

Ewan took note of her narrowing eyes and tightly drawn mouth and surmised that the surly guard was about to receive his comeuppance. "Lord Duncan isna laird. I am. Now pray leave us."

"As you will, milady."

His churlish look left no doubt as to what purpose he thought she meant to use that privacy. Ewan would have given an eyetooth for the privilege of slamming his fist into the man's ratlike face.

Seamus bowed and backed away. Ewan watched him go, mentally mapping out each step. He waited until he'd cleared the orchard, and then moved toward her. "Brie, is ought amiss? You dinna seem yourself."

She swung about to face him. "I think I may love you. Well, there. Now that's said and done, I'll leave you to your book." She turned to go.

Ewan reached for her before she could take more than a single step. He laid his hands on her shoulders and gently but firmly turned her around. "Say that again."

She swallowed hard. "I was sitting on a bench in the kitchen garden, plucking daisies of all things, and suddenly it struck me that I might well love you."

Ewan's heart swelled in his chest. Later he would wonder what could have possibly sparked such a momentous revelation, but for now, he couldn't find the curiosity to care. Brianna MacLeod "might" love him.

She released a sigh. "Well?"

"Well what?" he echoed, torn between amusement and tenderness.

"Haven't you anything to say on the subject?"

He drew up beside her, pretending to consider. "So you think you might love me, aye?"

She swallowed again and nodded. "Aye, I think I might."

"That's welcome news, Brie. For I'm verra certain I love you."

10

HANDS INTERTWINED, they made their way back to the castle, silent because there was little else to say, but so very much more to feel. They passed few people on the way. A scullery maid regarded them with lifted brows as they gained the corridor to their chamber. It was the first time they'd touched or shown affection outside the bedchamber. He was still her captive, after all. Only cradling her slender hand in his hadn't felt like a breach. It had felt very right—and very lovely.

Behind the bolted bedchamber door, Ewan lifted the last of Brianna's clothes, her shift, over her head and off. Dropping the garment to the pile on the floor, atop his own discarded clothing, he stepped back to feast his eyes on the bounty that was Brianna MacLeod.

He slid his gaze slowly over her, admiring her full high breasts, narrow waist and softly flaring hips. Long legs, slender yet strong, that seemed to go on to eternity, captured and held his attention. Remembering the feel of those thighs cinched about his hips, he felt a bead of moisture slide down the side of his cock.

He lifted his gaze to her face. "My God, you're beautiful."

The compliment had her redhead's fair skin turning rosy, the blush starting at her hairline and riding her slender throat downward to the high slopes of her breasts. She shook her head and dipped her gaze, as if suddenly curious to make a study of their toes.

"What, you dinna believe me?" He lifted her chin so she would look at him.

The misery in her eyes plucked at his heart. "My husband didna desire me."

The admission took him by surprise, but Ewan didn't pause to ponder his response. "Then he must have been blind or a fool or both, because you're the bonniest lass I've ever set eyes upon."

She shook her head and bent to retrieve her shift. Straightening, she held it against her.

"Nay, dinna hide yourself from me, sweeting." He gently unfurled her fingers and took the garment away. Dropping it on the floor, he turned back to her. "To hide beauty such as yours may not be a sin against God, but surely it must count as a crime against man."

More properly, to hide the light that was Brianna MacLeod was a crime against him, specifically. Were another man to look upon her thus, Ewan wouldn't think twice before running him through.

"You've seen me naked a time or two." He shot her a wink, hoping to set her at ease.

Emerald eyes lifted to his face. "That is a different matter. You…well, you are beautiful."

She really must have no notion of how very lovely she was. Running his gaze over her from crown to foot, he knew a fierce, savage pride. Come what may, for this moment and within these four walls, she belonged entirely to him.

"Ah, Brie, you may be laird and older than I, but you have a great deal to learn about life and love and what true beauty means. Here, let me teach you." *Let me love you.*

He vowed to delay his own satisfaction as long as he might, to satisfy her beyond anything she had so far experienced or imagined. Only then would he take his pleasure and spend himself inside her, not because she'd coerced him, but simply because he wanted to. Strong yet gentle, fair-minded and honorable as she was, he couldn't imagine a woman who'd make a better mother than her.

He ran his lips along her slender neck, dallying in the hot hollow of her throat and nuzzling the curve of her shoulder, skimming the delicate bones just above her breasts. The latter were milky soft and marbled with delicate blue veins. Tamping down his urgency, he took his time savoring her sweet scent and satin-smooth skin, treasuring the feel and taste of her, his chest swelling with pride when she gave up the last of her control with a soft sigh and angled her head to the side, entrusting her body to his care. He pushed the seal ring aside and palmed her, worshipping her fullness and shape, marking how her lovely nipples stood out proud and hard. Even though he'd yet to touch her there, the engorged flesh reminded him of strawberries, wild yet sweet. Mouth watering, he bent his head and suckled the pretty pink points, swearing he wouldn't stop until he made her moan.

She did, letting out a low keening, her fingers tearing through his hair. Smiling to himself, he backed her toward the bed. Hands on her shoulders, he bore her gently down upon the coverlet. "Brie, sweet Brie, you please me well. I canna imagine the man who would not be happy to look upon you thus." He shifted to straddle her, bracing his hands on either side of her. He looked down into her wide eyes. "Brianna...Brie." For whatever reason, he couldn't seem to get enough of saying her name.

He lowered his head to her breasts, tonguing each rosebud nipple and then drawing the sensitized flesh between his teeth before continuing on his path. Sliding downward, he turned his attention to her belly, trailing openmouthed kisses across the flat, moon-pale plane, pausing to tease her navel with the tip of his tongue. Brianna's moans deepened. Her hips lifted from the mattress and her fingers grew greedy in his hair, her nails raking his scalp and her fingers urging him closer still, lower still.

He went, not because he was her captive, but because he quite simply wanted to. Time stood still and worries over the future vanished like a Highland mist burned off by a scorching summer sun. His world, his very existence, shrank to what was happening between them in bed. He had no purpose other than to please her, nor did he ask for any reward beyond achieving that single-minded aim. He loved her and she might well love him. For the moment, nothing more mattered.

He moved down the length of her, laving kisses over her lower belly, crisp curls the copper color of late-autumn leaves teasing his chin. His whispered breath skittered across her mons, and she sucked in a heavy breath. "I can love you well, my lady, if only you'll give me leave."

He slid his hand between her closed knees and gently pushed her legs apart. It wasn't her sweet thighs she needed to open to him fully and freely. It was her heart.

He slid a hand beneath each of her knees and lifted her legs. Hooking her slender ankles over his shoulders, he bent his head and skittered kisses on the inside of each thigh. Slowly and steadily he moved toward her core, the prize. He found her lower curls to be damp with dew. The musky fragrance made his mouth water and his cock swell. Drawing back, he spread her wide with his fingers and looked down. Her swollen nether lips were berry-red and succulent as a ripe plum. Thick rich cream leaked from her slit and her clitoris stood out from its hood as if begging for his tongue. He felt her throbbing against his fingers, and smiled to himself. As much as Brianna might protest that physical pleasure held no sway over her, her body's passionate response showed otherwise.

"Ah Brie, I ken I please you more than you care to admit."

Holding her legs open about his neck, he bent his head and lapped her, milking her essence with his mouth, firming his tongue and striking it against the sheltered pearl of her passion, her clitoris, again and again. Not sheltered for long. He circled, teasing and then retreating to kiss her thighs, her curls, the sides of her knees, anywhere and everywhere save for the spot she craved.

Her restless head lifted from the fringed pillow. She

looked down on him, eyes desperate, pleading. "Ewan, please, I can't bear it. You're *murdering* me."

"Patience, Brie. Passion too quickly satisfied soon fades, whereas prolonging it increases the reward tenfold."

He continued his sensual assault, drawing out her torment, and with it his, too. Brie's bucking hips and clawing hands told him she approached her release. Her skin was flushed as if with fever, and when he slid a finger inside her, her inner flesh felt as scalding as a brazier newly pulled from the flames.

He knew the moment she let go. She came against his mouth, her woman's flesh quivering like a bow-string from which an arrow had just been released. He covered her with his mouth, her petal-soft skin flutter-ing against his lips and tongue, her keening cry filling his ears and heart with happiness.

He waited for the last quake to settle before gently returning her legs to the bed and drawing away. Looking up into her sweet, sated face, he realized she had no notion that the climax she'd experienced wasn't the end. It was only the beginning.

Throwing one leg over her hips, he straddled her. Finding her breasts with his mouth, he pulled on each of her nipples in turn.

"Ewan, I don't think I can bear any more." She made a feeble effort to shimmy away.

"Too bad, milady, for if I must bear the waiting, then must you bear the pleasure."

Still suckling, he reached down between them. She was drenched from her climax and more than ready for him. As much as he yearned to bury himself in the folds of swollen hot flesh, he held back. Whatever Fate held in store for them, he meant for Brianna to remember this moment for all time.

He captured her clitoris with the pad of his thumb, plucking her as though she were a lute. Caressing the swollen flesh again and again, he held his gaze on her lovely face, which was taut with both ecstasy and torment.

Brianna's eyes flashed open. Her luscious lips formed a shocked circle. Seconds later, she sent a scream swirling out into the chamber. She came again, this time into his hand. He squeezed her mound, absorbing each contraction as it rolled through her. When he finally pulled away, his palm and fingers were sticky with her nectar. He slid one digit inside his mouth, drinking her in.

The taste of her proved to be his undoing. No longer possessing the willpower to wait, Ewan mounted her, his cock finding a home in her heat. Tight and wet, she cinched about him like a glove. He loved everything about making love to her, the light floral scent of her skin, the little sounds she made when he was pleasuring her, the look on her lovely face when she begged him not to stop. He well knew what she wanted, craved, but a large part of giving it to her was making her wait—and beg. The begging was proving to be especially important.

Sliding out again, he stroked the base of his shaft over her rosy-red slit, not sure how much longer he might last or indeed how he'd lasted this long, and yet determined to drive her as mad as he might.

"Ah, Brie, never has a woman pleased me so well. You are the first lass ever I loved, as well as the only one. Marry me and make me the happiest man in Christendom." He'd meant to ask her later, but the present suddenly struck him as the perfect time.

Her hands fell to her sides, her fingers fisting in the sheets. Rather than reply with words, she lifted herself to him in silent appeal. As close to coming as he was, the rocking of her hips had him biting the inside of his cheek.

The image of her bending over to retrieve her shift from the floor shot into his mind. Inspiration struck and he slid his hands beneath her and flipped her over onto her hands and knees. She went readily, grabbing hold of the headboard and spreading her legs wide. Her beautiful buttocks shone pale as the moon, the firm lobes begging to be laved and later bitten. He gave the nipping kisses greedily, licking the sensitive spot at the very tip of her spine, driving her so wild that she butted against his mouth. Because he knew she could take it, that she was wetter and hotter than she'd ever before been, he reared back and drove into her.

Sheathed to the root, he felt perspiration rolling down his ribs. Never before in his life had he come so close to thoroughly losing himself in a woman. Truth be told, he wasn't close, but rather lost entirely, lost in the wonder that was Brianna MacLeod.

Breath hitching, he reached around and anchored his hands to her breasts, her nipples chafing his palms, his member swelling inside her. "Marry me, Brie." He brought her breasts together hard, but judging from her throaty cry, not quite hard enough to hurt. "I'll make love to you every morning and every night." He slid out and sank into her again, the slapping of their sweat-sheathed skin prompting his primal growl. "I'll never grow tired of loving you." Holding himself stock-still, he leaned forward and whispered in her ear, "I vow you'll be the happiest, best loved wife in all of Scotland." He withdrew yet again and slid into her with enough force to draw her gasp.

When she still didn't answer, he could only think she must be too lost to the pleasure to mark his meaning. Nor was she the only one in danger of losing herself to passion. The backward flexing of her hips was rapidly bearing him toward the breaking point. Before he broke, he meant to try one final time.

"Only think, Brie, to feel this pleasure every day— and every night." He glided one hand from her breast down the front of her, stopping at the moist space just above where they were joined. He lightly scratched his fingernail over her swollen clitoris.

A raw scream tore forth from Brianna's throat. She convulsed around him, her inner muscles milking him like a tightly closed fist. Her violent shuddering sent him plunging over the precipice in turn. Ewan finally let go and spent his seed inside her, the hot, hard contractions rolling over him wave upon blistering wave.

BRIANNA STRETCHED OUT beside Ewan, languid as a cat, and promptly fell asleep. Midday sunshine streamed into the chamber, bathing her lovely, long-limbed body in golden light, the sea-scented breeze wafting inside to dry the damp, red-gold tendrils curling about her flushed face. Propping himself up on one elbow, Ewan ran his gaze over her. She looked beautiful and whole, satisfied and sated, and altogether happier than he had so far seen her. A slight smile curved her lips, as though she must be in the midst of a delightful dream. She'd molded her lush, lovely body to his, laid her head in the curve of his shoulder and settled in to sleep beside him. For the longest while he lay there holding her, content to watch her sleep, at near perfect peace.

Not wholly perfect, for she had yet to answer his marriage proposal. Still, she wanted to make a baby with him, and Ewan no longer viewed her plan as the travesty he once had. He wanted children, sons to carry on after him, though a bonny little daughter with flame-colored hair would be nice, too. But he wanted more than to simply plant his seed and be on his way. He wanted to lie beside Brianna night upon night as she increased, rub soothing unguents into the swell of her belly, knead the ache from her back and make slow, gentle love to her, if not with his cock, then with his fingers and his mouth. He wanted to hold his newly born child in his arms and look down into Brianna's tired but radiant face, blot the perspiration from her brow and be a husband to her in every way.

He gave her a gentle nudge. "Brie?"

"Hmm?"

She rolled onto her side and he captured her against his chest. With one arm wrapped about her waist, he bent to her ear and asked, "Do you think we might have just made a baby?"

Her eyes remained closed, but he felt her tense against him. "I don't know. We'll have to wait and see."

He stroked his hand over the flat plane of her belly.

"You're so small and tight, it's hard to imagine you increasing."

"All women increase no matter how large or small they start out. I may not grow big as a croft, but I'll be big enough. Though I have hopes I may not waddle like a duck, at least not too badly."

The reference to his fair-day teasing wasn't lost on him. He grinned. "Brianna MacLeod grown so large she must sit still for once in her life. I'll need the proof of my own eyes to believe it."

Despite their banter, he felt his spirits dip. Assuming they were so blessed, he wouldn't have the chance to see her thus. By then he would be long gone, restored to his clan, according to the sad bargain they'd struck. He opened his mouth to ask her to marry him again, and then clamped it closed, not wanting to spoil the moment. But the unspoken words weighed like a millstone on his heart.

The damnable bargain they'd struck was proving to be a devil's pact, indeed.

SOMETIME LATER, Brianna turned on her side and feathered her fingers through his damp ebony hair. Even sated beyond her wildest imaginings, she couldn't seem to get enough of touching him.

"You're so beautiful, I think you must be a selky who's shed his skin and come onto land."

His lazy-lidded gaze met hers. He shook his head and smiled. "'Tis you who are the faerie creature spun from gold and moonbeam and sprinkled with rose petals." He fingered a lock of her red-gold tresses and twined the strand about her nipple, still swollen from his kisses.

For once Brianna was at a loss for what to say. The wonder of making love with Ewan after declaring their mutual love was like attending the end of a feast, expecting the beggar's portion of leftover bread sopped with meat drippings, and instead finding yourself in an honored seat, being served the finest milled bread and choicest cuts of meat. Not only her body but her heart was near to bursting with the bounty.

Ewan's husky voice called her back to the present. "You have a beautiful body, Brianna MacLeod." His hand left her breast and he smoothed it over the curve of her hip and buttocks, following the path with his eyes.

Once such a frank assessment would have brought forth a bevy of blushes, but the past weeks with Ewan seemed to have banished her sense of shame entirely. She met his crystal clear gaze and smiled. "I couldn't say. Whenever we're in bed together, I'm too busy looking at you."

It was no more than the truth. She adored him. When earlier he'd asked her to marry him, rather than spoil the mood, she'd bitten her lip. If only she might have answered "aye," how happy she would be. To live out her days—and nights—in Ewan's arms was her heart's desire. But for now any marriage between them must remain a cherished dream, a fantasy. So long as Callum stood accused of Donald's murder, there was no hope for making their union permanent. Mayhap it was her wishful thinking at work, but more and more of late she was coming to wonder if Ewan's brother might be innocent of Donald's murder, after all. Loving Ewan as she did, knowing the beauty of not only his face and form but also his soul, she found it hard to believe he shared blood with a murderer.

His faint smile broke into a broad grin of firm lips and beautiful white teeth, the same teeth that had nipped and nibbled her mere moments before. "Only looking, is it?" His teasing tone told her he knew exactly what she wanted to be busy doing.

Thinking of Alys's tragic tale, she reached for him, wanting to keep him close for as long as she might. "True, looking would be just the start. There would also be touching and tasting, too." She trailed two fingers down the thick muscle running along his throat, and then leaned in for a lick. His flesh was salt-flavored and savory, the most delicious of feasts. She drew him gently between her lips and teeth and suckled, no longer caring whether or not she left a mark.

"Hmm, you're rare tasty, too."

Drawing back, she held his gaze and smacked her lips, loving how easy it was to be playful with him, how free she felt simply lying in his arms.

He wiggled his eyebrows. "Dinna stop there, lady. All my parts are fair game when plundering lips are as sweet as yours."

"Unfortunately, I must. I have the council meeting to attend."

He cupped his big hand to the back of her head, bringing her closer. "Can you not be late?" His warm gaze promised a host of delights if only she stayed.

With regret, she shifted away and rose from the bed. "Nay, I canna. My privy council has requested this audience, and once granted, I canna deny it, much as I might want to." When one was laird, duty took precedence over pleasure.

Fortunately, in this case, pleasure need only be postponed. Ewan would be waiting for her when she returned. They could share a late supper and then retire to the bed she'd come to think of as theirs, and make love yet again. As hungry for Ewan as she already was, mayhap they'd miss the meal altogether.

Dressed, she turned back to take her leave. "I dinna ken how long this will take."

"It doesna matter." Gloriously naked, he got up and followed her to the chamber door. "Be it an hour or a day, I'll await your return."

Brianna tried to draw comfort from the sentiment, but foreboding found its way into her belly. This day she would return to find Ewan waiting, but what about the days and nights ahead?

BRIANNA ENTERED the small walnut-paneled chamber where generations of MacLeod lairds had convened their advisory councils. In the present case, however, it was her advisors who sought the meeting. The situation was unusual if not precisely irregular.

Though she was not late, Duncan and the other eleven old gentlemen of the clan were within already. She crossed the threshold, stepping into the sullen silence. The tension in the room hung heavy as the air before an impending storm.

"Milady." Standing at the front of the room, Duncan greeted her with his customary bow.

Defying creaking bones and gouty limbs, the other

council members pushed back their chairs and rose. Their gazes followed her as she made her way to the stone-topped round table and claimed her place at the head.

"My lords, I pray you be seated."

For the next few minutes, the chamber filled with the sounds of chairs scraping over stone floors and papers shuffling. Brianna seized the opportunity to take stock. The men assembled were all old enough to be her sire, her grandsire in some cases, but she reminded herself she was still their laird. Pulling back her shoulders and lifting her chin, she waited for them to resume their seats. Once the last had settled, she ran her gaze about the table once more, pausing to peer into each weathered face. To a man, they dropped their eyes when she came to them, never a good sign.

Dread settled into the pit of her belly. The fluttering in her chest increased from butterfly to dragon's wings. When still no one broke the silence, Brianna did so for them. "I feel as though I am among a colony of mutes. Come now, my lords, speak up."

Twelve pairs of eyes, including Duncan's, stared back at her. She felt their silent censor like a cold draft blowing across the room. Despite being a mature widow of almost five and twenty, she suddenly felt very young.

Seated to her right, Duncan turned to her. "A band of Frasers was sighted in the Cuillin Hills about nine leagues southwest of us."

Her heart skipping a beat, Brianna kept to her seat rather than vault out of it. "Do they carry heavy arms?"

Lord Angus, the wizened warrior at her left, spoke up, "Aye, milady, cannon and claymores."

So the Fraser meant to lay siege. Brianna didn't have to ask what they sought, or rather who. Callum Fraser was coming to claim his brother.

Addressing Lord Angus, she felt Duncan's gaze boring holes into her back. "How long before they reach the castle?"

She'd heard her father remark often enough that Angus had been a worthy warrior in his day. Though he must be nearing eighty, and was bowed of back and thin as a fence post, the faded blue eyes he lifted to hers were canny and alert.

The old man didn't hesitate. "By dawn, milady. Mayhap sooner."

Dawn. Brianna's drumming heart slowed, then stilled. Face hot, she snapped her head about and looked at Duncan. "Why was I not informed ere now?"

An uncomfortable silence descended. At length he answered, "You have been…indisposed of late. I did not wish to trouble you until I could confirm the rumor with my own eyes and ears."

By indisposed, he meant abed with Ewan. Brianna felt a surge of guilt and then struck it down. A knock outside her chamber door was all it would have taken to rouse her. It was almost as if he had deliberately delayed imparting the news until he could do so before her council, and thereby cast her in a bad light.

Fury washed over Brianna. "That was not your decision to make. Indisposed or not, in future I will expect to be informed at once."

"Of course, milady, I beg pardon." Expression rueful, he bowed his head.

His obsequious manner grated. By all accounts, Duncan had served her father faithfully and well. Beyond that, she'd grown up thinking of him as more of an uncle than a distant cousin. But in the few short weeks since she'd assumed the mantle of laird, she'd come to suspect his motives were not as wholly pure as she'd once believed. Her thoughts kept turning back to the day of Ewan's abduction. Duncan had laid the blame for his prisoner's condition on Ewan's struggling, and his son, Hugh, had corroborated his account. At the time Brianna had accepted their word, but now she was less sure. Thinking of the whip marks marring Ewan's beautiful back and shoulders, scars he would likely bear for the rest of his days, she felt a surge of guilt—and anger. Pride, her old sin, had held her back from asking him what had happened that day. She hadn't wanted to seem as though she couldn't control her own men.

Duncan's current actions showed just how far out of hand the situation had spun. By failing to inform her of the attackers' approach, he had placed everyone within the castle in the path of peril. Beyond its walls, there were the crofters to consider. There was no telling what pillaging Callum and his men might do as they advanced.

Duncan would have to go. She had been gainsaying her intuition for weeks now, but there was no denying the obvious evidence. For the present, though, she had a far more pressing matter to resolve than removing her privy councillor. She must deliver Ewan to his brother posthaste before any blood was spilled.

Throat thick, she pushed back her chair and rose. She prayed she would clear the room before the first tear fell.

"The captive must be conducted back to The Fraser before he and his men reach the castle."

Duncan's voice called her back. "There is another matter of like urgency to address."

Wishing the man gone already, Brianna frowned. "And pray tell, Duncan, what is that?" She glanced over to Angus, but this time the wizened warrior looked away.

"You should name a successor at once in case… aught should befall you."

"Your care for me is most touching, my lord." She didn't bother to soften the sarcasm underscoring her tone.

Apparently undeterred, Duncan sallied forth. "My son, Hugh, is a worthy and noble knight who has proved his worth in serving this clan willingly and well."

Of all the pronouncements Brianna had braced herself to hear, the shock of this one struck her dizzy. Gangling and pimple-faced, Hugh had only just celebrated his eighteenth saint's day. Moreover, it was abundantly clear the lad was a follower, not a leader.

"You want me to name Hugh as my successor? He is but a boy."

"Actually, milady, my proposal is that you should marry him."

A wave of dizziness struck her, making her glad to resume her seat. She had never before swooned in her life, not even during that first doomed pregnancy, but there was a first time for everything.

"Hugh is a fine strapping lad and yet tender enough in years to be malleable to milady's guiding hand—and mine, as need be."

So he meant to set up his son as his puppet. Digging

her nails into the table's edge, Brianna acknowledged that she didn't want a boy bridegroom. She didn't want a husband who was malleable, convenient as that might at times be. She wanted a husband who could be both passionate lover and loyal helpmate. She wanted Ewan.

These past days with him had changed her in ways both large and small. Thinking back to the sparring matches and love play they'd engaged in, she lifted her lips in a wistful smile. Even when chained to her bed, he'd still refused to give in, to cede so much as an inch. Since his less than auspicious arrival, he had challenged her at every turn to be the very best she could be as a laird and also as a woman. How could she settle for less?

She leveled Duncan a glaring look. "It is most… generous of you to offer up your son, my lord, but I must decline. A laird's marriage is as much an alliance as a union between a man and a woman. I see no value to be gained from plighting my troth with a fellow clansman."

"Alas, milady, should…*circumstances* require that you marry in haste, plighting your troth with a young man of an understanding nature might prove valuable indeed."

His mention of "circumstances" was a veiled reference to the possibility that she was with child. Though she'd yet to whisper a word to anyone, the queasiness she'd experienced these past few mornings brought to mind the early days of her previous pregnancy. It would be another few weeks before she could be certain, but she suspected her plan had succeeded—that she carried Ewan's babe in her belly.

"I am not marrying Hugh."

"I do not understand—"

"Silence!" For the second time in as many minutes, Brianna cut the older man off. "I am your laird. I do not require that you understand me, only that you obey me." Feeling as if steam must be spouting from her ears, she glared pointedly at the chamber door. "For now, make the necessary arrangements for one of our warriors to provide Lord Ewan safe escort to his brother's encampment this eve. Otherwise, consider this council dismissed."

11

WITH HER SPIRITS SINKING, Brianna returned to her bed-chamber, where a smiling lover and a sumptuous supper awaited her. Glancing from Ewan to the small feast he'd contrived, she considered it a great pity she hadn't the heart to do justice to either.

He closed the volume of *The Canterbury Tales* and smiled up at her. "You were gone a long time." He set the book aside, rose from his chair by the candle and crossed the rushes toward her. "I just finished 'The Parson's Tale.'"

She pulled the door shut behind her and tried for a smile. "Did you find it merry or sad?"

"Merry in the main, though Chaucer has a talent for finding humor in the darkest of situations."

Wishing she possessed a similar skill, Brianna glanced over to the table. The chess set had been moved, and in its place several pewter platters and a decanter of ruby-red wine were set out. A brace of candles occupied the table's center.

Following her gaze, Ewan said, "I hope you're hungry. There's food enough to feed an army."

An army, indeed. Brianna had never felt less like eating

in her life, but she smiled and nodded nonetheless. In the course of the past weeks, Ewan had broken down her every barrier, forced her to relinquish control, and accept pleasure and happiness as her due. It was a lot to give up, even if their parting turned out to be only temporary.

He turned and began lifting covers off the serving platters. Peering over his shoulder, she saw he hadn't exaggerated, at least not much. The salmon dressed with lemon butter and capers alone might have fed a family of crofters for more than one meal. Oysters steamed in almond milk, a salad of tender young lettuce and a platter of cheeses, nuts and wild fruits completed the bounty.

Forcing a smile, she rounded the table. "This is a feast indeed. However did you manage it?"

Ewan lifted the decanter and poured wine into the chased-silver chalices. "I whispered a word in Milread's ear that it was to be a celebration feast, and she had the girl, Alys, see to it all." He handed Brianna the wine cup with a gentle smile.

Her heart heavy, she accepted the goblet. "What exactly are we celebrating?"

"The future." He clinked his cup against hers.

Brianna took a small sip, though her heart wasn't in the toast. The wine, though sweetened, tasted bitter as gall. She set it aside.

Ewan put his down as well and reached for her hand. Lacing his long fingers through hers, he beamed at her. "I meant what I said earlier. I want us to wed, Brie, and the sooner the better. For all we ken, you may be with child already. I mean to clear my brother's name, but that could take awhile. I dinna want us to wait."

His fingers caressed the heel of her hand, tracing the thin ridge of scarring on her thumb. Even with her unshed tears building, Brianna shivered with the pleasure that light touch brought.

"Ewan, I—"

He held up his right palm to stay her. "You must ken you already have my heart. I've been wearing it on my sleeve for the last sennight if not before. Truth be told, I've loved you since first we met."

Ewan loved her. He'd said so earlier, but hearing it again sharpened the pain of their imminent parting to a dirk's edge. Bittersweet regret rolled over her. She loved him, too, so much that her heart throbbed with the ache of it. For the first time she rued the day her father had first told her he meant to name her as heir. She had chosen power over love, and fittingly, it was a bitter harvest she was reaping. Though she'd cared for Donald as her childhood companion and kinsman, she'd never really been in love with him. Her time with Ewan had showed her that loving a person and being in love wasn't the same sentiment at all. Now that she understood the difference, she'd give anything to be plain Brianna MacLeod, a woman who might wed for love and no other reason. But by her own design she was laird, The MacLeod. The lowliest crofter might give her heart where she pleased, but not Brianna.

With her heart in her throat, she watched him pull off the ring he wore on his little finger, red jasper set in simple gold filigree, the precious stone an age-old symbol of love.

Looking up, he explained, "It belonged to my mother.

Since her passing, I vowed I wouldna take it off my hand until I met the woman who would be my bride." His eyes stroked over Brianna's face, as tender as any physical touch. "I'm looking at her now. Marry me, Brie."

"Oh, Ewan." She shook her head. A sob caught in her throat.

He reached for her hand again and, turning it over, pressed a kiss into her palm. Looking up at her, his moonstone gaze struck hers. "I want you as my wife, Brie. I want to raise children with you and grow old with you, and share your tears as well as your smiles every day, every hour, of our earthly lives." He turned her hand back over and tried sliding the ring on her finger, but she snatched her hand away. "Brie?" His hurt gaze met hers.

Tears built in her eyes. The knot cinching her throat threatened to choke her. If only he knew how very much hearing his proposal pained her, not because she wanted to refuse him, but because she so desperately wanted to accept. She no longer wanted him as her handfast husband. Not a month, not even a year and a day would suffice to love him as he deserved. She wanted him for always and forever, because she loved him so very dearly, so very much. She had dreamed for ten years of being laird, but only now did she grasp what that meant. Sacrifice, self-control and, apparently, a cold bed and loveless life.

"Your brother and a small army of your clansmen are encamped not far from here. They will reach the castle by daybreak tomorrow."

Ewan sucked in a heavy breath. Blowing it out again, he said, "I will speak with Callum, explain how circumstances have changed."

Circumstances. That troublesome word reared its head yet again. "Beyond these four bedroom walls, nothing has changed, Ewan."

"Everything has changed. I love you and you love me. You pledged your love mere hours ago, as I pledged mine ten years ago."

"Ewan?" In the midst of her sorrow, confusion struck. Despite a decade's passage, Brianna's memory of their fair-day meeting was crystal clear. To be sure, they'd kissed and pledged to marry, but no words of love had been spoken.

Ewan knit his forehead. "My letters, Brie. My many letters, which you dinna see fit to answer."

He'd sent her letters? She shook her head. "Believe me when I say I never received so much as one line from you." One letter, dear Lord how precious that missive would have been. She didn't care to think her father had kept them from her, but given the outcome, what other conclusion could she draw?

Desolate, she shook her head. "I do love you, Ewan. I do. But that doesna change the fact that I've called your brother out as my husband's murderer. A laird canna be forsworn."

"Where does that leave us?"

Swallowing against the lump straining her throat, Brianna focused on holding her voice firm and her gaze steady. "I release you from our bargain. I have arranged for a guard to accompany you to the border between our lands. The horses are being saddled even now. You may leave within the hour. There is plenty of light yet and nay reason for you to tarry."

"Brie." He took a step toward her.

She stretched out her arm to stay him. "Dinna spoil it, Ewan. These past weeks have been so verra…lovely. I wouldna trade them for a king's ransom, and that is God's own truth. But the time has come for you to return to your clan and for me to carry on with my future." Tears building, she turned to go.

His voice called her back. "Then you are stronger than I, because I canna fathom a future without you."

She shook her head, wondering how much heartache she would be called upon to bear. "Ewan, dinna make this any harder than it must be."

"Brie!"

Throat thick, she hesitated and then slowly turned back around. One look at his stricken face sufficed to send her flying into his open arms.

THEY MADE LOVE SLOWLY AND sweetly, knowing it might well be the last time. Afterward they dressed and sat side by side, holding hands on the edge of the bed, their supper grown cold and untouched save for Brianna's cat grazing atop the table.

Ewan took her face between his hands, his big thumbs stroking away the tears. "I dinna know how to say goodbye to you."

Brianna tucked her head into the curve of his shoulder. "Then say 'until we meet again.'"

A knock sounded outside the door. A voice Ewan recognized as Seamus's called out through the paneling, "The horses are saddled and provisioned, milady. Hugh awaits Lord Ewan's pleasure."

So Duncan had deigned to send his son. Perhaps he was trying to make up for his earlier breach. For the time being, Brianna was too weary and heartsick to care.

Rising, she called back, "Lord Ewan comes anon." She turned to Ewan, who had risen to stand beside her. "Now wouldn't it be a fine thing if you were coming and not going?"

The tried-and-true Scots farewell ordinarily made for a humorous goodbye between host and guest, but in this case the parting might well mean farewell, and neither of them could muster much in the way of levity.

He laid warm hands atop her shoulders and shook his head. "We belong together, Brie."

"I know." She reached for his hand and carried it to her lips. "Hugh will see you safely to your brother."

Ewan nodded, the ache centering on the left side of his chest almost beyond bearing. "Callum didna murder Donald, Brie. I mean to prove it. I mean for us to be together."

She flashed him a quick nod and a falsely bright smile, but she was holding back tears, he could tell. "If anyone can do so, it is you, my love." He couldn't be certain, but he suspected she was humoring him. Switching subjects, she added, "There is something I would ask of you before you go."

Swallowing thickly, he nodded. "Anything, Brie. I'll do anything you ask."

She walked over to the carved chest and lifted the lid. When she turned back to him, she had his old flute in hand. "Mind how once you promised to play me any tune I fancied?" She held it out for him to take.

He lifted his gaze from the instrument and looked deeply into her eyes. "You kept it all these years? Why?"

She made a gesture of helplessness. "Before Donald and I wed, I took it out fair near every night before bed to look upon it and remember how once upon a time a boy's Pied Piper playing led me astray into a stable." She stopped, her slender throat working. "Play for me now, Ewan. One song is all I ask of you. Only let it be something soft and sad and suited to goodbyes."

She reached for his hand and pressed the length of smooth wood into his palm. Closing his fingers over it, she took a step back.

It had been years since he'd last played. With his heart in his throat, he took a seat on the side of the bed, moistened his mouth and then laid the flute against his lips. The song was equal parts sad and sweet. She stood watching him with tear-bright eyes and folded hands. Her face turned up to the light looked very beautiful and very sad.

When he'd finished, he stood and held out the instrument to her. "'Twas my gift to you, your bride gift."

His other gift, his mother's ring, he'd left lying on her desk. Were he to give it to her now, she would never accept it. He hoped she would happen upon it when the time was right and recognize it for what it was—a testimony to all that she meant to him.

Firming his voice, he added, "If you willna accept it as a token of my love, then seize it as a trophy not unlike those bull's horns you keep in cotton wool and bring out for feast days. Only in this case, keep it in remembrance of the fortnight when you held dominion over a Fraser, not only his body but also his heart."

EWAN WAS GONE. Even having commanded him to leave, Brianna found the reality almost impossible to fathom. She sat at the solar window, struggling to make peace with that irrefutable fact. He'd become so much a part of her life these past two weeks that she was hard-pressed to imagine how she would carry on without him. She would find a way, of course. Duty and possibly their coming child demanded it.

Why must it always hurt to love?

Before bringing Ewan back into her life, she might have settled into her widowhood with something approaching contentment. There would be no such complacence now. Like the mythical Pandora who'd succumbed to the temptation to open the lid of the forbidden box, thereby letting loose a swarm of evils upon mankind, Brianna found there was no going back.

She and Ewan said goodbye ten years ago as fair-day friends, strangers. This parting was different and achingly final. They'd eaten and slept and loved together nearly day and night for more than a fortnight. Brianna had started out by sharing her body and ended by relinquishing her soul. She'd grown used to Ewan lying beside her, to the book set out on the chest by the bedside, to all the myriad signs of his maleness scattered haphazardly about the once orderly room. She'd grown used to laughing and loving and occasionally arguing with him, to pressing her body against his in the middle of the night when she awoke cold. The feeling of missing him wasn't simply going to fall away. He'd only been gone a few hours and already it felt as though a year had passed—a long, lonely year of unrelenting winter.

This time, though, she strongly suspected he'd left her a gift far more precious than his flute. She ran a hand over her still-flat belly, thinking of the precious pearl she prayed was taking shelter in her womb. Whether the bairn was a boy or girl, born with black hair or red, she hoped he or she would inherit Ewan's crystal clear eyes.

Shouting drew her gaze downward to the tiltyard below and the two figures facing off on horseback, wooden swords at the ready. A page and a knight, his father, were engaged in a practice joust. She mentally replaced the short, stocky knight with Ewan and the long-limbed boy with their unborn son. The daydream progressed to the point where she included herself in the happy picture, greeting them as they returned from the tournament field, perhaps chiding their boy to wash his hands before sitting down to supper, then looking over his tousled dark head and sharing a private smile with his father—Ewan, her husband and the father of her other bairns, as well.

Had circumstances been otherwise, it could have all been so lovely, so perfectly whole and beautifully complete. Letting him go had broken her heart, the heart she'd boasted no longer existed. But Ewan had proved her wrong. Over the past few weeks, he'd made her feel again, want again, hope again. It was almost cruel how quickly she'd given herself over to him mind, body and, yes, soul. What had begun as fleshly lust had blossomed into something far more beautiful and lasting.

Her plan had progressed in perfect order, too perfect. Because of it, their baby would never know his father. Laying a hand over her belly again, Brianna vowed she would shower their child with enough love and devotion for two parents.

Mewing drew her attention down to the floor. Muffin looked up at her expectantly, his latest offering clamped in his mouth. Thinking it must be the usual bird or mouse, Brianna waited for him to drop it at her feet.

He did, the booty hitting the floorboards with a metallic sound. Dead things didn't as a rule "ping" like that. Brianna bent to retrieve it. Oh, my. Her cat had brought her Ewan's ring. With her heart in her throat, she slipped it onto her finger and held it up to the waning light. Had he left it behind by accident or design? she wondered. Ordinarily Brianna didn't put much faith in oracles or omens, but this once, she was tempted to believe the ring's reappearance must be some sort of sign.

Sometimes it wasn't enough to hold fast. Sometimes you had to believe.

Milread's words of a fortnight ago rushed back to her. *The stones foretell of a long and happy life, with one bairn soon on its way and a lusty, raven-haired husband to fill your belly with plenty more in the years to come.*

Brianna snapped her head up to find Alys standing in the open doorway, her expression wistful. "I hope I'm not disturbing you, milady. I just saw Lord Ewan ride out in the company of Lord Duncan."

Brianna looked up from the ring in her palm. "Lord Duncan? Are you certain?"

Alys didn't hesitate. "Aye, milady, 'twas him."

A funny feeling of unease fluttered in Brianna's belly, but she waved it aside. "I sent Lord Ewan back to his brother. I had no choice. The Fraser learned I was keeping him before I intended he should. As much as I wished to keep Lord Ewan with me, to do so would have brought about much bloodshed."

The girl hesitated and then stepped across the threshold. She opened her mouth as if to say something, and then closed it again.

Brianna studied her face. "What is it, Alys?"

"I probably ought not to say anything. In all likelihood, it's just my silly imagination but…"

Brianna was already out of the chair. "Tell me, Alys."

"The other day when your seal ring went missing… well, late that morning I chanced to see Lord Duncan coming out of your bedchamber."

Brianna's hand fisted about the ring. "Did he see you?"

"Nay, or at least I dinna think he did. He stopped to say something to the rat-faced guard and then went on his way."

The wheels of Brianna's mind began grinding at a frantic pace. Her seal ring going missing, then turning up in the same spot she'd searched for it. Callum Fraser's arrival in the area. Duncan's pushing her to wed his son. Ewan's letters from all those years ago, which had never found their way into her hands…. Coincidences, mayhap, but Brianna didn't think so. If her privy councillor was plotting, then she'd as good as sent Ewan off to his death.

"Alys, would you feel all right leaving Alasdair in Milread's care for two days, mayhap three?"

Alys chewed her bottom lip, considering. "I suppose so. He rarely suckles now. Solid food seems to satisfy him. And he's fond of Milread and she of him."

"In that case, go to my father's old trunk and bring out the two remaining shirts and trews. The boots will be too large to fit us, of course. We'll have to borrow a pair each from the pages."

The girl's high brow knitted in a frown. "But why would we dress in men's clothes, milady?"

"We will make better time on our journey if we travel on horseback, and the only safe way to do so is to travel as men. A litter would be slow going and prove too conspicuous. We require the element of surprise."

"Wherever are we off to, milady?"

"To fetch the father of my baby home."

CALLUM HAD JUST RETURNED from hunting his supper when one of his archers stationed in the trees reported sighting a lone rider coming up the mountain path. They'd chosen the mountaintop for their encampment for reasons both defensive and practical. The secluded spot afforded a bird's-eye view of the valley below. There was scant chance of an enemy sneaking up. The nearby copse was as well stocked as any game preserve and there was a freshwater stream nearby. They could replenish their water skins and hunt without depleting their precious food stores. Castle MacLeod was as solid as fortresses came. If The MacLeod refused to release Ewan, Callum fully intended to lay siege.

Senses on full alert, he handed the hare he'd just bagged over to a page, and reached for his broadsword.

Archers and claymore-wielding warriors assumed their positions, their captains awaiting his signal. He beckoned to the page, who handed up a lantern. Holding the light aloft, he squinted out into the distance. Something about the rider's straight-backed seat in the saddle and lean silhouette struck him as familiar—very familiar indeed.

"God's blood, it's my brother. It's Ewan." Heart pounding, he called for his men to lay down their weapons.

Several minutes ticked by and then Ewan emerged into the clearing. Watching his brother lead his horse up the rock-strewn path, Callum acknowledged he had never been happier to see anyone in all his days. Ewan hailed him. Callum dug in his knees and rode toward him.

When they met, Callum stared into the face that was a mirror image of his own. Almost. Whereas Ewan's eyes were light gray, almost clear, Callum's were a deep cerulean-blue.

Ewan looked about at the small army amassed. "This is a verra big gathering for a hunting party, brother," he said with a cocky grin.

"'Tis your rescue party." Callum drew back uneasily, half wondering if his brother might have suffered a blow to the head. But Ewan's crystal-colored eyes seemed as sharp as ever and he held his back lance-straight. Staring at his twin, Callum felt a sudden dull ache on the left side of his chest. It took him a moment to recognize the source—grief. His brother's grief.

"I didn't know I was in need of rescuing. Can a man not go off on a wee holiday without an army being raised?"

The question sent Callum's reserve tumbling like a

house of cards. "Damn it, brother, you've been gone more than a fortnight. When I came upon your campsite and saw it ransacked, what was I to think? And then I received a message from The MacLeod that she'd abducted you—"

"Brianna wrote you?" Ewan seemed surprised, and this time Callum didn't think he was playacting.

Callum opened his mouth to ask how he came to be on a first-name basis with the rival laird, but for once held his tongue. "Aye, for whatever reason, she seems to think I murdered her husband."

Ewan swung his gaze to him. "Did you?"

The question took him aback. Torn between anger and hurt, he shook his head. "I dinna. I never laid eyes on the clot. But even if I had, why would I want to kill The MacLeod's consort?"

"Someone did, and I mean to discover who."

Callum regarded his twin. He reached over and pointed to the stitch work on Ewan's shirtsleeve. "That's the MacLeod crest, is it not?"

His gaze slid away. "Aye, it is."

"Why is it, brother, I have the feeling there is more to this tale than you are telling me?"

Ewan's guarded gaze met his. He did not deny it. "Have you ever read *The Canterbury Tales,* brother?"

Callum scowled. "What does a bloody book have to do with you being kidnapped?"

"It is a most engaging book about journeys, though I'm coming to see that the strangest tales of all have yet to be written."

12

DRESSED IN HER DISGUISE, Brianna stepped up on the mounting block. A tug on her sleeve sent her whipping around. She turned to see Milread beside her, the woman's thin hand anchored to Brianna's arm.

"Send a messenger in your stead, milady, or better yet, send me. I'm no afraid of the Frasers. If I come to harm, it willna matter. I've lived a good long life. But for you, milady, it is too dangerous. Last night I dreamed an eagle flew over you whilst you slept, its great talons poised to strike your bonny head."

Though impatient to be off, Brianna hastened to reassure her. "Mind when you last read the runes, they foretold of a raven-haired husband and a bairn soon to come?"

Milread screwed up her shrunken face. "Aye, what of it?"

"I suspect I'm carrying Ewan Fraser's babe. The one thing I'm still lacking is the raven-haired husband. But I mean to go and fetch him home, if he'll still have me, that is."

The old woman released her with reluctance. "You use my words against me, milady, but I ken you've made up your mind."

"I have." Brianna swung her leg over the horse's side and slid her booted foot into the stirrup.

"In that case, I wish you God's speed, milady. I'll do what I can to ensure your safekeeping by tying a blue ribbon about a snipped-off strand of your hair. And yours, too, Mistress Alys."

Brianna turned to Alys. Mounted on a gentle palfrey, the girl was pale but seemed to be bearing up. "Have you ridden before, Alys?"

She hesitated. "Aye, but 'twas a donkey, milady, and only for a short while."

"This will be different."

Alys firmed her chin. "I will do my best not to hinder you."

"I know a back way, but you must swear never to speak of it. The safekeeping of everyone biding within the castle depends on your silence."

Alys's pretty face sobered. "I swear on my dear Alex's grave I'll no breathe a word to anyone."

"In that case, follow me." Brianna turned her horse to the northwest and the beach.

Rock beds surrounded three of the four sides of the castle base, one of several reasons the castle had withstood siege upon siege over the years. Be the enemy a rival clan, marauders on the lookout for loot, or their age-old enemy, the English, none had succeeded in breaching the awkward slopes below the thick stone walls.

At the northwestern quarter, however, a curved flight of stone steps descended to the sea gate that had served as Brianna's childhood hideaway. The secluded entrance had a practical, defensive purpose as well. It afforded inhabitants of the castle a built-in escape route.

They slowed their horses to a walk, picking a path through the rubble. Brianna glanced back over her shoulder to her companion. Even for a seasoned rider, the plunging cliff presented a daunting prospect. Predictably, Alys's face was ashen and her blue eyes wide as saucers. To her credit, though, she kept her seat, her lithe body straight, her white-knuckled hands holding steady on the reins, her pursed lips not opening to utter so much as a single protest.

"You're a braw lassie, Alys, even if you are a Lowlander." She shot the girl a wink before turning back around.

Alys called back, "Ah well, milady, after birthing a bairn fair near the size of a sow, anything seems simple."

Judging by her unaccustomed queasiness and aching lower back, it was beginning to look as though Brianna might soon be testing the truth of Alys's words. She'd always preferred working out-of-doors to performing household tasks such as stitching altar cloths and shirts for the poor, but improbably, she found herself looking forward to her lying in—assuming a certain raven-haired warrior was still willing to wed her. After the tumult of the past fortnight, and the daunting journey that lay ahead, embroidering tiny bull's horns on a baby's smock and having a handsome husband rub her feet while she did it would be all the adventure she required.

HAVING TAKEN HIS TALE up to the point where he'd given Duncan the slip, Ewan rode in silence beside his brother.

Since the day of his capture when Duncan had taken such delight in wielding the whip whilst the other two warriors pinned him, Ewan had suspected Brianna's privy councillor was not the honorable man he showed to the world. What he'd lacked was proof. When at the last minute Duncan had stepped in to replace his son as Ewan's escort back to his brother, the leaden feeling of foreboding landing low in his belly wouldn't be denied. It was his warrior's instinct screaming to him to retreat. The older man's stopping to relieve himself had afforded Ewan the very opportunity for which he'd been waiting. As soon as Duncan dismounted, Ewan dug his heels into his horse's sides and raced away.

His body might be bound for home, but his heart, like his thoughts, were very much with Brianna. She might have released him from his fetters, but he was as much her prisoner as he ever was.

They'd traveled for about an hour when it struck him that he was behaving like a clot head. A man would have to be soft or addled to walk away from a woman like Brianna simply because she told him to. His love was not only as stubborn as he, but also noble natured to a fault. Beyond that, he was honor-bound to tell her of his suspicions about Duncan. He would have done so ere now, but his shame at being beaten by a graybeard had held him back. What a fool he'd been!

Once the blood feud was ended, Brianna would have no further reason to refuse his suit. He didn't want to be handfast for a year and a day. He wanted her as his wife for however many years God might grant them together. He loved her. Looking back, he realized he'd loved her since that faraway first meeting in Fife on fair day. Sometimes when you met your soul mate, you just knew. He fancied she loved him just as fiercely. What else really mattered?

"I'm verra sorry, Callum, but I have to go back."

The black scowl his twin shot him would have cowed a lesser man. "Back? What the devil for?"

"To fetch my bride."

He turned his horse's head and spurred the beast back toward MacLeod lands.

HIDING HIMSELF AND HIS horse in the copse, Duncan watched Brianna and her insipid little maid lead their horses along the rock-strewn path. Though they'd set out before him, the maid wasn't much of a horsewoman. Their slow going quickly placed him in the lead. He hadn't had to guess where they were headed. Like a bitch in heat, Brianna MacLeod was chasing after her man.

To bide his time, Duncan reflected on the past frustrating months. It occurred to him that Ewan's escape might be a blessing in disguise, for it freed him to go after the grander prize: Brianna. Poisoning Magnus, former MacLeod laird, numbered as the first of several plots that had run amok through no fault of his. Unfortunately, the poison he'd slipped into Magnus's meals had taken longer than it should. The laird was a hearty, hale man who, until Duncan began dosing him, had never spent a day ill in his almost sixty years.

Still, Duncan had schooled himself to patience. He'd dared not increase the dose too drastically. A rapid decline was bound to spur suspicions. He'd always had the feeling that Brianna's old nurse, Milread, saw a great deal more with her clouded eyes than she let on. On several occasions he'd caught the crone staring after him as though she knew exactly what he was about, her gaze seeming to monitor his every move for all that she was supposed to be blind.

The particular poison he'd chosen was supposed to have a paralyzing effect. In its final stages, it robbed the victim of his power of speech. Once again he'd been disappointed. The laird had retained his faculty of speech up to the very end, not to mention his stubbornness. He'd named Brianna his heir before all twelve members of his council, including Duncan, and then promptly closed his eyes. He'd been making noise in that direction for the better part of ten years, but Duncan hadn't really believed he'd go through with it.

Duncan had been wrong.

For someone who'd been waiting in the background for decades, it was almost too much disappointment to bear.

All Brianna need do was produce a healthy boy and Duncan's dreams for Hugh would be as good as lost. For that reason, he had pushed for her marriage to an idiot like Donald. Reliable rumor had it that Donald fancied pretty young pages. Unfortunately, the bloodstains on the bridal sheets the following morning showed he was also prepared to do his duty by his bride.

Donald had had to go. Laying the blame for his death at Callum Fraser's door had been a convenient bit of stagecraft. According to Fraser tradition, the new laird must make a pilgrimage to the monastery of Saint Simeon. Persuading the haughty young lad to strip down to his shirt to do penance had taken some doing, but in the end the monk Duncan had bribed, Brother Bartholomew, had prevailed. Once he had the garment in hand, it had been a simple matter to tear off a small strip, later to be used as "evidence."

Donald hadn't hurried off to the loch to meet with Callum Fraser, as he'd broadly boasted, but to tryst with his latest paramour. When Duncan had approached instead, the young man's shock had been palpable. The daft man had been so busy sputtering excuses that he'd never once asked what Duncan held behind his back—a rock that he brought down upon his victim's silly head. Afterward, he pulled the scrap of Fraser plaid out and stuffed it into Donald's stiffening fist.

Eliminating him had been the easy part.

It was Brianna who made things hard. The girl had been the bane of his existence from the day she'd been born. Her fair-day flirtation with Ewan Fraser had caused him no end of trouble. He'd intercepted any number of lovesick messages before the boy finally gave up. In persuading her father to "hold fast" and marry her off to Donald, Duncan thought he'd had her settled at last. Given her husband's…*proclivities,* he'd been shocked when she turned up pregnant. Still, there were herbs well known to bring on a woman's flow. When the first stab of pain struck, everyone, Brianna included, had blamed the miscarriage on the shock of Donald's death. Duncan had hoped she might die, too, but like that mangy feline she kept, Brianna seemed to have nine lives and the devil's own luck.

Duncan fully intended to see that The MacLeod's luck—and her life—ran out this very day.

IT WAS COMING ON DUSK by the time Brianna and Alys crested the mountain leading to the main road. Woods surrounded them on either side, the close-growing trees blocking out sun and moon alike.

Alys suppressed a shiver. "'Tis like the witch's forest children are warned against wandering into." She rubbed her upper arms as if chilled. "If it's all the same to you, milady, I'd as soon press on and make camp once we're out in the open once more. They cannot see us but we canna see them, either." She cut her wide-eyed gaze from left to right.

"They?" Brianna asked.

"Aye, the night folk, milady."

Brianna was less worried about ghosties and goblins than she was mortal men. Secluded areas such as this one were natural haunts for thieves. The very last thing she needed was to run afoul of a band of outlaws or poachers.

A sense of unease gripped her. Icy fingers trailed along her spine and she shivered, though the air was more cool than cold. Alys was not the only one of them who would be relieved to reach the other side.

Picking their way through the dark made for slow going. Brianna had ridden this way a time or two with her father. On those occasions it had never occurred to her that she wasn't safe. The copse was deeper than she remembered it, but then no doubt she and her da had been engaged in some lengthy discourse that had passed the time. Hoping his strong, loving presence might be guiding her now, she nodded and pressed onward.

Silence fell as each woman slipped into her own private thoughts. Though the catalyst for her setting out was to intercept Ewan and hopefully persuade him to take her back, Brianna's quest went beyond securing her personal happiness. Even if she proved to be pregnant, it wasn't fair to expect an unborn child to do her work for her. It fell to her as laird to confront Callum Fraser and demand to know what had passed between him and her husband. She should have done so weeks ago. Instead, she had accepted the report of Donald's murder from Duncan and his two guardsmen. If Ewan's brother had murdered Donald in cold blood—and she was beginning to have her doubts—then let him look her in the eye and say so.

Either way, she was not about to let the opportunity pass. She had brought a white linen handkerchief with her and would find a stick upon which to tie it. Once they neared the Fraser lands, she would wave her makeshift flag, the universal signal for a truce. It was time for the feud between the clans to end once and for all. Too many innocent lives had been ruined or lost.

They reached a clearing, and Brianna turned to Alys. Picking their way through the bracken and closely growing trees seemed to have sapped her. Head bowed and shoulders slumped, the girl looked as though she might slip out of the saddle at any time.

Brianna pulled up on the reins. "Let us stop for a wee rest. The horses look like they could do with some water, and if memory serves me, there is a stream just ahead."

In truth, the animals would be fine for several more leagues and so would she, but the little maid looked near to dropping.

Alys dragged her exhausted eyes to Brianna's face. "Well, if you ken the horses need a rest, then I suppose I might climb down and stretch my legs a bit."

Brianna hid a smile. "That sounds like an excellent suggestion. I think I will join you."

They dismounted. Brianna took over care of the horses and sent Alys on ahead to the stream to fill up their water skins.

She had just finished securing the reins to a low-hanging branch when horse hooves sounded in the near distance. Cocking her head, Brianna was almost certain the approach was that of a single rider. Her heart leaped, carrying with it her hopes. Ewan? As soon as the thought arose, she dismissed it. He and Duncan had several hours' lead on her. Besides, she'd sent him away. He would have no reason to believe she had changed her mind and come after him.

Duncan walked his horse into the clearing. He drew up and dismounted. Watching him, she felt a sinking sense of disappointment—and dread. How had he known she was here? And where was Ewan?

"Where is Lord Ewan?"

Tethering his horse, he shrugged. "With his brother." He left his mount and strode toward her. "It isna safe for women to travel without male escort." Drawing up before her, he didn't bother bowing.

As much as Brianna wanted to believe him, she didn't, not fully. His weathered face wore a wooden look, and his stony gaze had her worrying. Old though he was, he was also a big man with a barrel chest and fists the size of twin haggises. She had never really given much thought to his size and strength before now, but it occurred to her that she was very much alone. Still at the stream, Alys was too far away to hear her call, and they were several leagues from the main road where other travelers might happen by.

Resolved to brazen it out, Brianna pulled back her shoulders and straightened her spine. "That is none of your affair, milord. I shall send word if I have need of you, but I assure you I am perfectly fine. Pray dinna let me delay you on your journey home."

Drawing up before her, Duncan shook his head. "You always were a headstrong lassie, too headstrong for your own good. Your father spoiled you by letting you run wild as any lad, and because of it, you think you're the equal of a man. If you'd kept to a woman's proper place, you would have saved me a great deal of trouble." He slid a hand to the knife sheath at his waist.

Brianna caught her breath and backed up. The waning light glanced off the smooth metal of the dirk he brandished. Thoughts racing, she recalled that her own small dagger was tucked into her boot and out of reach. Frantic, she darted her gaze about, searching for something else to use as a weapon.

He swung toward her horses and slashed through their tethers. Letting out a shout that would have raised the dead, he slapped the lead horse on the rump. The stallion shrieked and bolted, the palfrey following.

Duncan advanced on Brianna, blade at the ready. "I

was sorry to have to send your father to his heavenly reward before 'twas his time. We'd been friends from our youths and he was a bold warrior, a good man. Loving your mother made him soft, though, weak. And then you came along." Duncan spat.

Brianna couldn't believe her ears. The man must be mad. "My father died of natural causes. He was ill for many months."

The man grinned. "Aye, he was ill, but the cause wasna natural."

Panting, Brianna backed up another step. It took several heartbeats before the implication of his words sank in. "You poisoned him, didn't you?"

"Aye, and I would have done the same to that codless scut you wed, only there wasna time to let the herbs work their magic."

"You killed Donald, too!" Her scattered thoughts circled back to Ewan. Dear God, had she sent him to his death in truth?

As if reading her mind, Duncan shook his head. "The Fraser dog cut and run. No doubt he is with his whelp of a brother by now, your kisses a fast fading memory."

Ewan had escaped! Sweet relief flooded her. It must be true. Braggart that he was, Duncan wouldn't hesitate to add another man's death to his grisly trophy list. Whatever else happened, Ewan at least was safe.

She, on the other hand, was anything but.

Perspiration broke out on Brianna's forehead. It was coming on night. In another few moments, it would be fully dark. Duncan would murder her, and afterward, Alys. Like as not, he would find some way to lay the blame on Callum Fraser's doorstep yet again. Ewan had insisted his brother wasn't a murderer, but she'd refused to listen. God's blood, what a prideful fool she had been.

"Before you kill me, at least tell me why you killed Donald." She supposed it didn't really matter at this point, but the longer she kept him talking, the longer she had to live.

He stopped in his tracks and met her gaze, looking almost proud. "With your da dead, I couldna very well have you siring sons, now could I? Your death would have drawn too much suspicion, but your consort was…expendable. Not so now. With you out of the way, I shouldna have any great difficulty convincing the council to name Hugh as laird."

"I wouldna be so certain of that were I you," she retorted.

His face darkened. "Once word of your stabbing spreads, there will be those like your crone, Milread, who will consult the stars and the runes and conclude there must be a curse on your house. The people will be more than willing to have my son as laird."

"You are a monster." It was too dark to clearly see him beyond the whites of his eyes and the gleam of his blade.

He didn't bother to deny it. "'Tis time we said farewell, Brianna." He closed the last of the distance between them.

She backed up and bumped into something solid— a tree. The back of her head thumped against the trunk and she winced.

Duncan laughed. "You disappoint me, milady. I had expected better sport from you. It seems killing you will be fair near the same child's play as withholding your lover's letters ten years ago…." He raised the knife.

Horse hooves thundered toward the clearing. "What the devil…" Distracted, Duncan wheeled around.

Brianna seized her opportunity. She lunged to the side and ducked, dragging the dirk from her boot. Her fingers curved around the jeweled handle, and she leaped up in time to see something big and heavy land atop Duncan. Caught in its clutches, Duncan crashed to the ground and rolled.

Squinting, she saw that the "something" wasn't a wild beastie but instead a man. Relief hit her. She stood in a half crouch, knife at the ready lest she be called upon to join in the fight. At present, it was too dark to differentiate her savior's form from that of Duncan's. Then the moon cleared its bank of clouds, shedding crystalline light upon the men deadlocked at her feet. She looked down and caught sight of her would-be rescuer's dark head and broad back. Her heart hitched and her stomach plummeted.

Ewan!

13

THE MEN ROLLED, kicking up dirt, Duncan struggling to keep possession of the knife and Ewan struggling to wrest it away. A few vicious jabs had the blade coming dangerously close to Ewan's eye. Looking on, Brianna held her breath. Grunts, groans and labored breaths filled the still night air.

Duncan bared his teeth. "You should have left well enough alone and gone back to your cursed clan while you still could, Fraser."

Ewan had the older man's left arm pinned and was working on his right. "What, and miss out on the pleasure of killing you?"

"I dinna ken I'll be the one to die this day."

A jab to Ewan's solar plexus won Duncan the top position. Brianna gasped. She steeled herself to tackle Duncan and plunge her dirk in his neck.

Then something whizzed past Brianna, so close she could feel the breeze by her ear. She looked down. Dark though it was, she could make out the arrow sticking out of Duncan's back.

EWAN SLID OUT FROM beneath Duncan's slack form and stood. Bypassing the dead man, he came up to Brianna and enfolded her in his arms.

Tucked against his damp chest, she wrapped her arms about his neck and hung on for dear life. "Oh, Ewan, you came for me? How did you know Duncan followed me? He murdered my da and Donald both. He would have murdered me had you not come."

He exhaled a heavy breath into her hair. "I didn't know. I was riding home with my brother and his party when it struck me that everything I love lay in the opposite direction."

For the first time it occurred to her that he didn't carry a bow and arrow. Looking over his shoulder, she spotted a mounted man riding into the clearing, shouldering a hunter's longbow.

Coming up beside them, the archer tucked an arrow back in its quiver. "There is no need to thank me. You may consider it my wedding gift if you like."

Shadowed though it was, Brianna saw the newcomer had Ewan's dark hair and identical lean face.

Ewan turned to Brianna. "Allow me to present my brother, Callum, The Fraser. Brother, behold Brianna, The MacLeod."

Callum swung out of the saddle. Grinning, he caught Brianna's gaze. "I'd say it's high time we met, aye?"

Brianna turned back to Ewan. "You never mentioned the two of you were identical."

That seemed to strike him as funny. "We're not, at least not exactly. Though you'll have to wait for daylight to appreciate our differences." Sobering, Callum drew up before them. "I didna kill your husband, my lady, but I expect you ken that by now?"

Brianna nodded. "Aye, I do. That one of my own clansmen fashioned this feud pierces my heart. I don't know what to say beyond I'm sorry. Whatever recompense you require of me, I will do my best to make it."

Callum shrugged. "What's done is done, but the future is ours to set to rights as best we may. By the by, you're bonnier than I'd expected."

Brianna couldn't help smiling. These Fraser twins were charmers, to be sure. Yet even had she not already fallen head over heels in love with Ewan, his brother wouldn't have moved her in that way.

"So are you, though you should know I'm already spoken for—by your brother." She lanced Ewan a warm look.

Callum tossed his dark head back and let out a hearty laugh. "I like you, Brianna MacLeod. Let us go to my castle and end this damnable feud with a feast."

Brianna hesitated. Her own castle was no farther than Callum's. Beyond that, someone needed to bring Duncan's body back to the castle. She meant to make certain it was clear to all just who the murderer was.

She shook her head. "I thank you, but I canna possibly accept. I must see that yonder villain's body is brought back to my people. I want no doubts as to what truly happened."

Callum frowned. "I can send the body with a few of my men."

Brianna dug in her heels. "I thank you, but to do so is my right and duty as laird."

The two brothers exchanged glances. Suddenly Ewan grabbed hold of her and swung her up into his arms.

"We'll send one of Callum's men back with a message, and keep Duncan's body in the icehouse. In the meantime, have no doubt, Brie, you are coming home with me."

WATCHING EWAN HAUL The MacLeod off to his waiting horse, Callum shook his head. Imagining the manner of wooing his brother must have in mind, he was glad Brianna MacLeod was such a sturdy, strapping wench. Ewan was clearly besotted. Glad to be free of love's coil himself, Callum started to walk his horse toward the stream, thinking to rest awhile.

"Milord?"

He swung about to find a fair-haired beauty looking up at him, her golden curls tucked beneath a lad's feathered cap. She'd crept up on him quiet as a cat. Even sheathed in shadows, there was no mistaking her as female—and a fetching female at that.

Intrigued, he slid his gaze over her, taking note of her nipples poking through the saffron shirt and the way the tight-fitting trews shaped her slender waist and hips.

As if anticipating his question, she said, "I am The MacLeod's handmaid." She dipped into a curtsy that would have done a noblewoman proud.

"What name do you go by, lady?"

He'd expected her to flinch or at least step back from him. She did none of those things. "I am called Alys, milord." Straightening, she tilted her head and looked him in the eye.

Callum felt a grudging respect. He'd known knights who'd cowered when he'd addressed them in a similar tone, and she was but a slip of a girl. "Can you ride, Alys?"

He'd asked the question based on practical concern, but the prospect of her slender arms and tiny hands tucked about his waist flooded his loins with heat.

Her beautiful eyes narrowed. "I *was* riding, milord, until my mount and that of my lady were set loose." Her expression conveyed she thought him a fool.

Feeling foolish indeed to be so affected by a woman he'd only just met, he hoped she would spare him a similar perusal. Without looking down, he was keenly aware of the bulge tenting his trousers.

He started to stoop to offer her a hand up into the saddle, but she stood so much shorter than he that method would never work. Instead he slid his hands about her supple waist and swung her up into his arms.

Her hat fell off. Golden curls streamed around her face. Squirming, she shoved her small hands against his chest. "What…what are you about? P-put me down at once."

Looking into her adorably flustered face, Callum felt his heart turn over. Tenderness rushed through him. Without thinking, he reached down and brushed golden strands back from her eyes. Her skin felt flower-petal soft beneath his fingertips. Quieting under his touch, she stopped struggling and settled into his arms with a sigh.

"Better?" he said, not certain what he was asking, but hoping she would know.

She nodded slowly. "Aye."

Her eyes searched his face, a promise of heaven to come. What color were they? he wondered and vowed to soon discover that about her and much, much more. He dropped his gaze to her mouth, the shape of a perfect rosebud, and swallowed hard, more than halfway ready to kiss her.

He somehow found the will to hold back. Such reserve wasn't his usual way, but he sensed the slight lassie in his arms was a most unusual girl. Tamping down his regret, he lifted her onto his horse.

"Until we find your mount, you will ride with me."

"SURELY THIS IS HARDLY the way to celebrate the end of a feud."

Brianna glared up at Ewan from the bed to which he'd bound her. Instead of manacles and chains, he'd used silk scarves to lash her wrists to the bedposts. The gleam in his eyes told her he was greatly enjoying the view.

"Oh, I don't know about that." He cocked his head to the side. "Turnabout is fair play, think you not?"

Brianna felt her anger begin to build and with it, excitement. "You're…you're gloating."

Standing above her, he rolled his beautiful broad shoulders in a luxuriant shrug. "And if I am, who has more right than I? How many days was it you kept me chained to your bed?"

"That was only because I couldn't trust you not to try and escape."

One dark brow lifted. "And I suppose I can trust you?"

Brianna had no ready retort to that. She satisfied herself with a scowl.

"You're every whit as stubborn as I, as well as a fair hand with a dirk. Betimes, after the merry chase you've led me, it pleases me to see you thus. If ever a woman wanted tying up to free her from the weight of her modesty and self-possession, it is you."

"What is that supposed to mean?"

"It means that I want to make love to Brianna MacLeod, my future bride, and not the MacLeod chief. The latter has been banished from this bedchamber until daybreak." He bent and braced his palms on either side of her shoulders. Bringing his face down to hers, he stopped just short of kissing her. "You're in *my* castle, Brianna. You're as good as my prisoner, for the day at least. I am within my rights to use your body as I wish. *Any way* I wish."

Desire roughened his voice. The husky promise of dark delights to come had Brianna shivering.

He joined her on the bed. Kneeling over her, he reached for the front of her shirt. Not bothering with buttons, he tore open the front. "Ah, that's better." He pushed the rent cloth aside and brought her breasts together.

Looking down at her rosy nipples standing straight up, Brianna felt a shock of heat hit her face—and her sex. "You're a brute, Ewan Fraser." She tried to look serious, or better yet, afraid, but her smile kept breaking through.

"Aye, I am."

He rolled her right nipple between his thumb and forefinger. At the same time, he dipped his head and took her other breast with his mouth, his tongue rolling over her, his teeth nipping. Brianna moaned, wishing her hands were free, not to shove him away, but to rake her nails down the smooth skin stretched over his back and buttocks.

He reached for the front fastening of her trousers and tore the flap aside. Resting back on his ankles, he yanked the garment down her legs and then off. "Prisoner" though she was, Brianna lifted her hips to help him.

His eyes grew bright with a wicked gleam. "Tell me you don't want me."

Sensing this was but part of the game, Brianna looked him in the eye. "I don't want you."

"Liar. The cream running down your thighs tells me you want me well enough." He slid his hand between her legs and squeezed. "You're wet for me, aching—admit it."

Brianna sucked in her breath, desire striking hard and heavy where he grasped her. "I admit nothing."

"In that case, it is time you owned who is master here." He found her vulva with his fingers, and sliding them over the slick cleft, said, "I will pleasure you, pleasure us both, whether you will or no, and when I finish with you, I will ask you again to be my wife and this time the answer you give will be yes."

"If you have me now, like this, it will be rape." It wouldn't be, of course, but Brianna was warming to the game.

The smile he flashed her was worthy of a pirate. "Oh, I don't think so. The dew on my fingers and the musk filling my nostrils tell me you want me."

He slid two fingers inside her at once, the sudden

invasion trapping the breath in her lungs. The pleasure-pain radiating out from her sex to her limbs had her opening wider to accommodate his hand.

She sucked in a heavy breath and lifted herself against him. "Ewan…please." The plea wasn't for him to withdraw, but to join his buried digits with a third.

Gaze riveted to her sex, he suddenly seemed as lost to the moment as she. "So warm and wet and lovely you are, Brie. You make my mouth water and my cock stand. Now spread those sweet thighs of yours wider still and give me leave to enter."

He let her legs slide down the length of him and, wicked as she was, she took advantage of the freedom to knead the bulge in his trousers with her toes. He groaned and shoved her legs open, then shifted to straddle her. He trailed kisses over her breasts, her belly and the tops of her thighs, while his thick fingers moved inside her in new and wondrous ways, each stabbing thrust stretching and filling her.

She knew the very moment when his third finger entered her. The result wasn't pain but a deep, possessive ache. Wetness slid down her thighs. The pressure building inside her was almost beyond bearing.

She lifted her head from the pillow and looked down upon his dark head, her eyes filling with tears and her heart overflowing with love. "Oh, Ewan, you are my husband already in all but name, my love in every way."

"And you mine."

He settled his head between her spread thighs and took her with his mouth. The sensation of his tongue fluttering against her sex, combined with the hard fisting, brought Brianna to the brink.

The climax ripped through her, as swift in its violence as a summertime storm. Suddenly it was upon her. She was lost to it, with no recourse but to ride out its rage. A scream tore forth from her throat, and she came hard into his mouth, her inner muscles convulsing around his hand, the orgasm radiating out to her fingertips.

She returned to her body, wrists rubbed raw from straining against the scarves, throat hoarse from screaming. Ewan withdrew his hand and slid up the length of her. After sweeping slick digits over the seam of her lips, he leaned down to kiss her.

"Brie, sweet Brie, I almost lost you today. Games aside, will you abandon that pride of yours and consent to be my bride?"

Brianna swallowed hard. She loved him with all her body and mind and heart. Her wrists might be bound by silk, but her heart was thoroughly chained by her love for this big gentle man.

"If you're verra sure you want me, then yes, I'll marry you."

The smile breaking over his handsome face was as blinding as any solstice sun. "In that case, my laird and lady wife, let us be married without delay. I willna have any bairn of ours be ashamed of his parents once he— or she—learns to count the months."

Brianna started to tell him her suspicion that their child was already on its way, but his clever mouth found her again, doing those wickedly lovely things. His warm breath blew over her sex, his tongue striking a very special spot. Helpless against the pleasure only he could bring, she sank back against the pillow. Suddenly it was as if everything that had ever run afoul in her world had been set to rights, cleansed in some beautiful, mystical, magical way. Caught up in the swirl of sensation, in the wellspring of love she felt for this braw generous man, she gave herself up to the glorious pleasure of full possession, complete submission and long-awaited peace.

CALLUM FRASER WAS FEELING restless, and he couldn't say why. On second thought, he hadn't been himself since he'd lifted the girl, Alys, into his arms and onto his saddle. The ride home with her sweet little body molded to his back had been bittersweet torment. Once at the castle, he'd turned her over to his housekeeper's care. Though he hadn't seen her since they'd parted ways, he'd dreamed of her all night.

His footsteps led him to the walled rose garden. In his mother's day, it had been a lovely place, but years of neglect had rendered it a ruin. He hadn't bothered coming here since his mother's death. If truth be told, he hadn't thought about the garden in years. Picking his way through the weeds, he sat down on the stone bench. A single rosebush had survived to grow wild in the corner. The partially opened buds put him in mind of a certain lady's perfect mouth. Callum had never been a slave to sentiment, but he found himself reaching out to stroke one fragile blossom.

As if his fantasy had conjured her from air, Alys approached. Pulling back his hand, he wondered if she'd seen him enter, and had followed him. The possibility made his pulse race.

"My lord." She greeted him with a slight smile.

In the daylight, he saw that her eyes were blue, the color of cornflowers. On his orders, suitable clothes had been found for her. Dressed in a simple blue gown, with a light muslin veil draping her golden tresses, she looked as though she'd stepped out of one of the stained-glass windows in his chapel.

She halted several paces before him, the purity of her face and form stealing his breath. "I do not mean to disturb you…."

He rose up from the bench. For the first time in his life, he had cause to wonder if his shaking legs would support him. "You do not." He took a step toward her, for she suddenly seemed much too far away.

"I am in search of my lady. I have not seen her since yesterday. Can you tell me which chamber she occupies?" She nibbled her bottom lip and cast her gaze downward.

Her modesty disarmed him as other women's wiles never had. He wondered if she was always this shy, or if perhaps, after the other day, his presence discomfited her. The latter thought roused his hopes, daring him to dream.

"I expect she is with my brother. In his bedchamber," he added, not out of necessity, but because he was curious to see if he could make her blush.

She did not disappoint. Pale roses nearly the same shade as her mouth climbed the trellis of her delicately boned cheeks.

"Shall I take you to her?"

She snapped up her head, her eyes registering what

looked to be alarm. "Nay, she and Lord Ewan have their own affairs to settle."

Callum chided himself for teasing her. It amazed him that he who had boasted that his body did not possess so much as a single sentimental bone could feel so completely tender toward this one wee woman. His heart swelled every time he looked upon her. Other parts of his anatomy swelled, too, but that sensation wasn't nearly as novel. None of his past dealings with women had left him feeling this way before. He yearned to lay her upon the bench, pull down the thin dress and suckle her small perfect breasts, and then push her legs apart and tongue and taste and tease her woman's flesh before he finally entered her, a climactic conquering possession. At the same time, he longed to take her in his arms and settle her on his lap and simply hold her, to tuck her head beneath his chin and shelter her against his chest like the rare treasure she was.

"Nay worries, lady, he willna harm her. Unlike me, my brother is the kindest and gentlest of men." For whatever reason, Callum felt the need to warn her away from him.

She sent him a puzzled look. "You do not think of yourself as kind?"

He hesitated and then admitted, "Not always. Not usually." True hunters always gave their quarry a sporting chance.

"You do yourself a disservice, sir. I think you're one of the kindest men I've ever met, and the noblest."

Callum couldn't recall the last time someone, a woman, had defended him. Never, he supposed, but then he wasn't the sort who deserved defending. "You dinna ken me well." She didn't know him at all, but still, it wasn't in his nature to be noble.

She stepped closer. "It's not every man who would put his own affairs aside so selflessly to search for a brother gone missing. Nor would any man be so quick to forgive the woman who had abducted and held that brother. And yet you treat milady and…and me as though we are your honored guests. A brute would have made us his prisoners."

He took a step toward her, shaking his head. "I ken you are one of those rare women who see only the good in people. And you are so very young." He kept his arms at his sides, not trusting himself to hold off from touching her.

She focused her gaze on the ground. Long lashes tipped in gold cast shadows over the tops of her fine-boned cheeks. Still looking down, she shook her head. "Not so, sir. Young and ignorant though I am, I have seen aplenty of that which is bad."

Her eyes filled. A tear slid down her cheek. Im-probably, Callum, who had never before been moved by a woman's tears, found himself completely undone by that single crystalline droplet. He lifted his hand to her cheek. Her skin felt satin smooth against his palm.

"How now, lady, why the tears?"

She shook her head. "You treat me as a lady because you are so good and kind, but I am not as I seem. I have a son. His name is Alasdair. Even though his late father and I were duly wed, no good household would take us in. I plied the harlot's trade to keep us."

The misery in her eyes and the trembling of her lower lip cut through the last cordon of Callum's self-control. He stroked his knuckles down her jaw to her chin. Tilting her heart-shaped face up to his, he looked into her eyes. "It seems to me you are a mother who so loves her child that she would sacrifice her own good for his."

She made no move to step back. Her mouth curved into a small smile and she shook her head. "Now which of us is determined to see only the good? And yet you say you are not kind, my lord."

He leaned in, his mouth hovering but a hairsbreadth from hers. As much as he wanted to kiss her, though, he wanted more—a great deal more.

"I have not always been kind. In the past I have been prideful and boastful and selfish to a fault. I have bullied and blustered and seized what I wanted without thought or care for the consequences. But with you at my side, sweet Alys, I believe I could be a better man."

"My lord?" Her startled eyes met his, posing a silent question.

Rather than answer it with words, he bent his head and set about coaxing open the perfect rosebud of her mouth with a gentle yet insistent kiss.

Epilogue

THE WEDDING TOOK PLACE a week later in the MacLeod chapel. The Fraser bridegroom and his best man, twin brothers, were startling alike in looks, tall and broad-shouldered, handsome and raven-haired. More than one guest from the MacLeod side remarked that it was fair near impossible to tell the two apart. The one true distinction was the extraordinary color of the bridegroom's eyes. Like moonbeams or starlight, Lord Ewan's gaze shone with an otherworldly clarity.

In contrast, their laird and her lady-in-waiting, lovely lasses both, couldn't have looked less alike. The bride was flame-haired, full-bosomed and nearly as tall as her new husband, whilst her handmaid was fair-haired, delicate and slight as a fairy.

Of course, it was Brianna's day.

She wore her lustrous waist-length copper curls loose and adorned with a wreath of ivy and herbs laced with blue satin ribbons. Her gown was of a shimmering bridal blue, the low-cut bodice sewn with pearls and gold silk thread. After the ceremony, she tossed her nosegay of dried flowers and sweet-smelling herbs into the throng of eager-eyed maids, and then descended the marble chapel steps on her new husband's strong arm. Amidst a shower of grain and snowflakes, they led the procession of guests, MacLeods and Frasers both, into the ivy-and-evergreen-bedecked great hall, where the feasting would commence.

Hours later, Brianna and Ewan drew back from the bride cakes stacked on the dais table between them, as well as from the clapping hands, bawdy shouts and lively strains of fiddle music rising up from the guest tables filling the hall below. They'd just managed the feat of kissing over the cakes without toppling them. The custom was meant to bring peace and prosperity to the newlyweds, but with the ending of the feud between their clans, that happy purpose already had been met.

Upon Brianna and Ewan's return to the MacLeod castle, the remaining eleven members of her council, shamed at having been so easily duped by Duncan's treachery, had pledged oaths of fealty to Brianna and Ewan, her consort. Angus was unanimously named to take Duncan's place as privy councillor. Rumblings that a woman was unfit to lead were no more to be heard.

It was harder to know what to do about Duncan's son. Hugh had sworn on his life that he'd known naught of his father's villainy. Casting himself at Brianna's feet and kissing her hem, he'd looked so distraught that she'd almost believed him—*almost*. Still, when she'd received the news that he, along with Seamus, had disappeared in the middle of the night, she couldn't help but feel relieved. Likewise Duncan's accomplice, Brother Bartholomew, had been dispatched. Presently, the bearer of false witness resided in Brianna's draftiest dungeon cell. Not even the monk's considerable girth would shield him from the northwesterly wind when it blew. She supposed she would release him someday, though certainly no sooner than spring.

With the feud ended and the last bitter reminders of the painful past months banished, the castle once more felt like a home—hers and Ewan's. Much like the sugary tower topping the table, the future rose up before them filled with the sweet promise of a lifetime of wonderful moments to be cherished and savored.

Nor were they the only lovers to reap the benefits of the new peace. Brianna leaned over to Ewan, resplendent in a cream-colored doublet shot with thread the same quicksilver color as his eyes, and whispered, "She might not have caught the bouquet, but I wouldn't be surprised if Alys and a certain Fraser laird don't follow us into the chapel ere long." She tilted her head to indicate the main table, from which they'd recently risen.

Seated near the head, Callum carved a sliver of capon from his platter and offered it to Alys. With a shy smile, she took a tiny bite and then held the remainder to his lips. Since their bizarre meeting the week before, the pair had been inseparable. Other than rising to lead the wedding toast earlier, the Fraser laird had stayed by his lady's side as if held there by an invisible chain.

Shaking his head, Ewan admitted, "I hadn't thought my brother a marrying man, but it seems miracles do happen."

"Aye, they do indeed." Thinking of her own yet to be announced "miracle," Brianna reached up to adjust her wreath from slipping down the back of her head.

At Milread's insistence, all the ingredients for a

long and happy marriage—sage for constancy, rosemary for faithfulness and thyme for fertility—had been woven about the willow-branch circlet. Thyme, at least, proved to be an unnecessary ingredient, for Brianna was indeed pregnant.

Shifting her gaze back to Ewan, she said, "One miracle in particular is due to arrive in nine months, give or take." She slid her hand down to her still-flat belly and smiled.

Ewan's eyes flashed and his jaw dropped. "Brie, is it so, truly?" He reached for her—and plunged his arm into the cakes.

Brianna jumped back, but not quickly enough. Like the biblical Tower of Babel, tier after tier of cake crashed to the floor, splattering her slippers and skirt in snowy frosting. A crack of collective laughter greeted the gaffe, and after a moment's pause, Brianna and Ewan joined in.

Sidestepping the mess, Brianna rounded the table to her bridegroom, his ears tipped in pink, one sleeve of his doublet covered in white icing. "Aye, my love, it's sure I am—and so verra happy." Heedless of his sticky state, she reached for him, her heart full with all the love held within.

She took his handsome face between her hands, his red jasper ring a reassuring weight on her finger. Who would have supposed that a boy's flute playing on a long-ago fair day would bring about such a bounty of blessings?

Blinking away grateful tears, she said, "Miracles do happen. Granted, not every day, or even as often as we might wish, but in the end, it is enough."

Ewan lifted Brianna's hand from his cheek. Turning

it over, he pressed a kiss to the fresh scarlet scar banding her thumb, and smiled at her. "As always, my lady laird speaks true. It is enough—and so verra much more."

Silhouette®

SPECIAL EDITION™

NEW YORK TIMES BESTSELLING AUTHOR

DIANA PALMER

A brand-new Long, Tall Texans novel

HEART OF STONE

Feeling unwanted and unloved, Keely returns to Jacobsville and to Boone Sinclair, a rancher troubled by his own past. Boone has always seemed reserved, but now Keely discovers a sensuality with him that quickly turns to love. Can they each see past their own scars to let love in?

*Available September 2008
wherever you buy books.*

SSE24921

LAURA WRIGHT

FRONT PAGE ENGAGEMENT

Media mogul and playboy Trent Tanford is being blackmailed *and* he's involved in a scandal. Needing to shed his image, Trent marries his girl-next-door neighbor, Carrie Gray, with some major cash tossed her way. Carrie accepts for her own reasons, but falls in love with Trent and wonders if he could feel the same way about her— even though their mock marriage was, after all, just a business deal.

**Available August
wherever books are sold.**

Always Powerful, Passionate and Provocative.

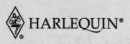

MARIN THOMAS
A Coal Miner's Wife
HEARTS OF APPALACHIA

High-school dropout and recently widowed
Annie McKee has twin boys to raise. The
now single mom is torn between choosing
charity from her Appalachian clan or leaving
Heather's Hollow and finding a better future
for her boys. But her handsome neighbor and
deceased husband's best friend is determined
to show the proud widow there's nothing
secondhand about love!

**Available August
wherever books are sold.**

LOVE, HOME & HAPPINESS

REQUEST YOUR FREE BOOKS!

2 FREE NOVELS
PLUS 2
FREE GIFTS!

HARLEQUIN®

Blaze™

Red-hot reads!